PICTURES FROM '

PICTURES FROM HOPPER

NEIL CAMPBELL

SALT

CROMER

PUBLISHED BY SALT PUBLISHING

12 Norwich Road, Cromer, Norfolk NR27 0AX United Kingdom

© Neil Campbell, 2011

The right of Neil Campbell to be identified as the editor of
this work has been asserted by him in accordance with Section
77 of the Copyright, Designs and Patents Act 1988.

Printed and bound in the United Kingdom
by Lightning Source UK Ltd

Typeset in Bembo 12 / 13.5

ISBN 978 1 84471 830 6 paperback

1 3 5 7 9 8 6 4 2

For FTP

CONTENTS

CARS AND ROCKS

I LIVED ABOVE Larry Flynt's on Broadway, just across from a bar called Vesuvio's. I could see it from the window of my apartment, and at night if I looked at the sidewalk under me I could also see down the tops of $50 hookers. I'm originally from a family of farmers in Salinas, and I got the Greyhound over to the city for a bit more life than you can get out of a hundred square miles of cabbage patch.

I worked afternoons in Vesuvio's, pulling pale ales for the tourists tired of sea lions and trams. When I wasn't busy I looked out of the window at the workers trailing up and down Columbus, saw their dumb faces, and knew I always hated that shirt-and-tie jive.

A guy who used to come in regular was the least famous in a family of actors, the son of one of the greatest actors in American cinema. He worked bit parts in the movies, mostly did theatre. Last time I saw him he was doing a Sam Shepard play at the Magic, and he used to come in to wash down tequilas with beer.

I was cleaning shot glasses, not looking at him, when I heard him stop in mid-flow. I looked up and could see his face backing away from me. The stool landed with a bang and his head cracked on the floor. If we'd had cameras I could have watched it again. Half an hour after the ambulance had taken him, twenty-

1

five women from an institute in Copenhagen came in, most of them wanting pale ales.

I met Alba on Rexroth and bought her some Corso in City Lights. With that and a Guinness or two in Specs she seemed to be getting in the mood. That changed when she saw the hole I was living in: the junkies' needles on the stairs, the paint-stripped door, the mess inside. I'd change the sheets only when they started to stink, I'd wipe dust when it got me to coughing. The bathroom I don't want to tell you about. So she asked me to walk her home, all the way up Russian Hill. Flat she shared with someone else I didn't know about then. Nice view up there after the fog: the boats in the bay, the bridges Bay and Golden Gate, the hills of Marin County. I stood in the doorway, kissed her, and she went in and I was left looking at the Golden Gate twinkling its way to Sausalito.

Alba was from Champaign, Illinois, and looked like a young Diana Ross. She always wore hats, beautiful hats, red, green, black. Put them on the bed. Did lots of drugs, got me down that road. She wore skirts like belts and boots up to her thighs and when she danced I lost the name of days.

Now I don't know if craziness always comes with beauty. I mean, I'm a good looking guy, or I was. Think *Cool Hand Luke*, only with eyes more blue. Not really. I was more like George Kennedy, big burly mother going bald. But with beauty there's all that envy, none of the girls like you, whatever way you look people think that *you think* you're better.

She liked me for the poetry. She wrote it too, in a way of speaking. One time we saw Ginsberg and Burroughs, another time Baraka at a bookshop on Irving. But you couldn't expect a poem to write one. She loved it though, and we'd walk around North Beach, sit in the park near the church, lay down on the grass in the summer. Sometimes we'd float stoned in the mornings, see the Chinese doing Tai Chi in the fog.

One day in Golden Gate Park, a man in a top hat went by on silver stilts. He carried a golden radio with an aerial going way up into the purple sky. Sea lions came wriggling through the grass and watched as we made our way through sparkling candy stars.

Alba told me her daddy used to pistol-whip her and slash at her legs with whipcord. She said he put her mother's head through the window and slit her fingers with slivers of glass. She told me her daddy used to rumble in and unbuckle his pants but not to hit her. I didn't swallow any of that windy city bullshit until I felt the welts on her legs and it made me shiver with visions. Sometimes when we made it she whimpered his name and I went at it harder to shut her up. One time right there she said she was going to kill me. She was profiled with the sun through the window and light steamed off her. She slid a fingernail across my throat like a cutlass.

An old trick of Alba's died and left her a little wooden home up above Cannery Row. Far enough away from the tourists, with a view of the Pacific, and the fish smells nothing like they used to be. Some days I'd sit in the window and see whales, just glimpses, but I got to recognize the splash of the tail and the way it moved in the water.

We'd go down there together, long walks along

the coast. In Monterey you could see otters, herons, whales, sea lions, all in the same cross hairs. And we'd walk down along Pacific Grove and freak the health nuts. The sea in Pacific Grove swirls and swirls in big waves and currents, the waves crash in big crashes of white, sometimes the water looks like a kind of jellied green in the dusk. We'd walk along the sand, nobody else around, eating strawberries and looking for galleons on the sea.

They hated Steinbeck when he wrote that book, but not when it brought the tourists in. You know the main character, Doc? His real name was Ricketts and there's a statue of him just up from Cannery. People put flowers in his hands. You can see the pacific over his shoulders. There's a bench right there. I'd sit with Alba and we'd watch tourists get to the end of Cannery and turn around for some plastic souvenir.

Alba. I thought I saw the Pacific in her eyes. One time I grabbed her arms and she clawed at mine. Put the nails into me, ripped right down. I didn't feel it then. I'm from a generation that don't hit women. I took it until one time we were in a car in Big Sur. I'd told her about the cliffs and the waves that they don't have in Champaign, Illinois. And I told her about Henry Miller. I pulled over near the Bixby Bridge and we got out, and she stood there shouting. It was 2:19 a.m. She started pushing at me, clawing again. I was protecting myself, not even looking, when I saw her face and body falling away. She broke up on the rocks. I tried to get back on my own. Couple from Abilene saw me.

I had my drinking days, waking up in alleys in the Tenderloin, groping around for a glinting bottle, getting up shaking to beg. I don't back-up from winos. I listen to what they say, give them a chance; tell them about the Shrine of St Francis of Assisi. Most will talk your ears off with the same self pity. But they're broken down. And who should we feel sorry for, them, or the women?

TEXAS WILDFLOWERS

BLACK EYED SUSAN

I woke up in a Super Eight and she was licking whisky off my stomach. I'd gone to write an article on a music festival and never went back. I lived with her in Austin for a while, then we moved to Houston before ending up in Tulsa, Oklahoma, once the oil capital of the world.

We didn't work much because she had this house of her own in North Tulsa. We sat on the porch on warm nights drinking coffee and smoking. In the afternoons we'd make love to the sound of freight trains. Once we rolled in a field of bluebonnets.

Friday nights we'd go out to Cain's Ballroom, and sometimes Susan got called up on stage to play fiddle with a band called the Catoosa Brothers. Cain's Ballroom opened in 1924 and on the way in there were big pictures on the walls of Bob Wills and his brothers. He was known as The San Antonio Rose, and his band the Texas Playboys. They called the music western swing, and they still play him on the jukebox between bands. I loved the one called 'Sittin' on Top of the World'.

Black Eyed Susan had this real slow drawl of a voice like the words were all leaning on each other. Once I got used to driving on the right we bought a battered Cadillac and went on a road trip to Fresno to stay with Susan's son, Lance. We listened to great American music as we kicked up dust over the plains: Freddie King, Townes Van Zandt, Mose Allison, even a little bit of JJ Cale, who lived over in Escondido.

SPANISH DAGGER

She came from the border town of La Rosa and made art derived from Kitaj and Kahlo. She had a big nose and big thick lips and the gold brown colour of her body and the sounds she made turned me into a bigger man than I knew I was. When she spoke Spanish with friends I could listen to them all night, just sipping my beer and relaxing to the sounds of that beautiful musical language.

There are all things in poetry more than facts. Like paintings that never leave you. There are colours and sounds and moods and feelings that even poetic words cannot describe. These things are contained in paintings, in the sounds of the Sea of Cortez, in the sunlight through the petals of chocolate flowers and the green sepals beneath them like eyes.

SILKY CAMELLIA

This crazy fireball came from Zona Norte via El Paso. The night I saw her on the street in Tijuana her red heels seemed to float over the dust and she was a black fire of oil in the neon heat haze. We drank tequila off each other's lips in a little cantina, where bearded men wrinkled with brown cut deals in the back or just sat

7

in the evening heat watching as flying creatures died in the blue light.

Camellia had a baby with brown eyes and he was looked after by his grandmother, a big woman in broken huaraches fondling a rosary, sad eyes like tiny chapel crosses. Camellia said the father wanted her to get it vacuumed. His brown eyes were wise in the cradle. Her place was so small he was only round the corner and when I went past him he was frowning and shaking his head at me in a way that meant he didn't need speech. She said he'd be in college one day, said her life in cantinas and on the streets would pay for it. I see her still, in lamp lit rooms, where the rosary hangs over the lampshade and red words blink in the window, and the crucifixes on the wall glint silver reflections on the sweating backs of gringo cowboys.

HUISACHE DAISY

They were fish scales under sleeves, white pins laid out over light blue, crisscrossing desert roads barren under red sun and blue skies of aeroplanes falling. They said help me. The temporary red messages slipped away, were blotted, flushed. Picking scabs became picking stitches, punching fists swollen by broken tables in the burned out nights at the bar. Looking good and living fast she kept them under her phone. Chemicals came after. It was too much for me to see. It kept her going and that's terrible and true. She's red ray petals on the bed sprawling over cream.

DAMIANITA

Damianita was from Lubbock, home of Buddy Holly and Texas Tech. When I landed the job there I'd never slept with one of my students before. I was filling-in on an English class. They assumed I knew all about Shakespeare. Because all English people are experts on Shakespeare, right? I went in with an umbrella for a joke. Waffled on about Hamlet, like he's the man who just thinks all the time, that thought is the enemy of action and all that. I pointed out that lots of people get killed in the play. Anyway I was playing a role myself—twirling the umbrella around, spouting patchy quotations—when Damianita raised her hand and said that an unexamined life isn't worth living. I stopped for a second and saw her as I see her now: the golden yellow hair, the slender body. I had to throw the umbrella into the air and catch it to return to my previous shaky train.

The next day she was ten years older and taking charge. By Thanksgiving she was getting bored, by the time summer came around I was altogether too old for her and ready for a break myself. The last time I saw her was in a bar where they were doing a poetry reading. She walked in on her own and was about the only girl there. I was worried a second but she smiled at me as she passed and sat down by herself. Poets came smiling towards her and walked away with nothing. At the end of the night a biker filled with piercings and tattoos came in holding two helmets and she smiled at me and shouted, 'Bye boys!'

MOUNTAIN LAUREL

I met Mountain Laurel at Texas Tech, too. She was from Pittsburgh. Big chin and big brain and big eve–rything. Big eyes that changed colour with the light. Went back with her for a week one time. Okay it was winter, but bare trees by the long bare roads, and closed down steel mills and mills still open pouring smoke into the already low clouds, those things made me want the bright consumables of Warhol, and then after that a drink, and then after that a walk down to three rivers, Monongahela, Ohio, Cleveland. But once that was done there was only more beer and recurring memories, and we sat at a roadside dive in the shadow of the interstate while she told me about rope swings and local boys and how she developed her precocious talents reading Richard Hugo and James Wright. When her parents were out I saw the bedroom she grew up in and the books of hers still there. The room filled with incense sticks and pictures of poets Robert Frost and Sylvia Plath and Ann Sexton. And she was all the time searching to develop herself in the way of young women, wanted what she got from me, and I remember her in vividly pale displays and how she was all the life of Pittsburgh, and for a while all the life of Texas Tech too.

DEATH VALLEY

I moved out to California. Went on my own to Death Valley and camped at Furnace Creek. There had been a lot of rain that year and Badwater was briefly changed from a squalid trickle of chloride and sulphates to a long lake glistening in the blistering sun. In the shadow of the Armargosa and Panamint Ranges, beneath the bulk of Telescope Peak, I walked through miles and miles of coloured fields. Beside the creosote and mesquite bushes I noted blues and purples of larkspur, purple mat and Mojave aster, golden California poppies, desert lupine and purple chias, Spanish needles, scarlet locoweed and desert five spots. I met a park ranger who showed me long caterpillars on the stems of the flowers. He told me of the increase in small lizards and rodents, the boost to the food supply of coyotes and hawks. He said that soon it would all be gone.

THE LIGHT ON
OCEAN AVENUE

There was black bruising all over Delmore's right fist, red across his eyes and puke around the rim of the toilet. He watched as the light in the window turned from bright to fading orange, and his mind was filled with the Hank Williams lyric, 'the moon just went behind the clouds to hide its face and cry.'

When they gave him his stuff back he got on a Green Line, and put his headphones on to listen to a shuffle of Hank Williams' *Greatest Hits*, *Greendale* by Neil Young, *Modern Times* by Bob Dylan, and *The Rising* by Bruce Springsteen. He looked down and flexed his bicep, changing the contours of the name 'Marisa'. Outside, under the grey sky, thin trees skipped by like a finger across pickets.

The bus moved down Ocean Avenue. Delmore got off and stood on the boardwalk. By the railings, an old man in a wheelchair sat looking out to sea. Nearing The Stone Pony, Delmore saw Chrissy signing for a delivery. He followed her in through the side exit. It was dark and the only light came from the front window that showed the grey horizon.

'Jesus, Delmore.'

'No, just Delmore.'

She put a bottle on the bar and he sipped it in the

dark while she continued to supervise the delivery. On the tables there were cardboard posters advertising upcoming gigs. Delmore looked at the glow of his phone in the dark, a number once burned in his mind now a name in a list of contacts. He sipped from his beer and kept looking at the number before starting to write a message. His finger hovered over the 'send' button, and he put the phone on the bar.

Chrissy put some of the lights on and Delmore squinted his eyes.

'You look like shit.'

'Thanks, sweetheart,' he answered, tilting forward his empty bottle.

He picked up his phone and pressed 'send', then took a big gulp of beer.

'How about some music?'

After a few minutes Springsteen's *My Hometown* came on.

'Hey, turn this up.'

He listened to the music and waited for his phone to vibrate on the bar. It didn't. Chrissy didn't say anything when he got up off the stool and left. On the boardwalk the man in the wheelchair was still looking out to sea.

Delmore put his hands in the pockets of his jeans, feeling the small change on the right side. A cold wind came in off the sea and ran through his long thinning hair. He wanted some warmth and his legs were done with walking.

The pier casino was gutted and derelict; a pile of greenish rubble still waiting to be swept away. Delmore's heart rose like it used to at the sight of a Ferris wheel. Her long hair was swirling in the sea breeze.

They got in Marisa's Subaru and drove out of Asbury Park to her house further down the coast in Neptune. Both smiled when 'Be My Baby' by The Ronettes came on, Delmore tapping his hands on his legs and Marisa singing along.

'She's got some voice, that Ronnie Spector.'

'You said it, Delmore.'

They walked into Marisa's house and she hung up their coats. 'I'm going to make you some tea, so you sit yourself down and I'll bring it in.'

Delmore walked over to the stereo and looked through her albums. 'Okay if I put some music on?'

'Yeah, go ahead.'

Flicking though her collection he picked out *The Best of the Crystals*.

With 'Then He Kissed Me' on in the background, Delmore and Marisa sat beside each other on the settee.

'What am I going to do with you Delmore?'

'Hey, what can I say?'

'Well, let me tell you. You need to make some changes or else that's it, for me.'

'Changes?'

'Yeah, changes. It's not occurred to you? I mean look at you. You're old, man. Hey, I'm old too.'

'You look great, though' he said, though he thought it funny how you were always still attracted to people your own age. Ten years before, the bags under her eyes would have dissuaded him. But he was going bald.

'This takes time,' she said, and he looked at her hands: the tidy, painted nails, the smoothness of her palms. He thought of them grasping his hair when he buried his head in the perfume of her breasts. 'What

I mean is that you've got to stop, maybe even go to a meeting.'

'I know. But I need you. I can't do this on my own.'

'Okay, well, just talk to me.'

'You know I've always been shy. It just made me more sociable. Life was boring without it. You're right, and I've had enough, but I've been doing it for thirty years and nobody has shown me anything better.'

'What about me?'

'Well, yeah, but.'

'Look, we're not married anymore, remember?'

'What I need is something *better*. I know it has made me *feel* better nearly every day for thirty years, but all I've been doing for thirty years is the same thing.'

'Well, look, like I said before, I need you to go to a meeting.'

On the phone he was still in denial and they explained to him the problem with that. But he didn't like it in these pampered times that everyone seemed defined by a disorder. He thought it was something people used as a badge in the hope that it made them more interesting. What had happened to his heroes from the movies, men like Robert Mitchum? They'd lived a life without restraint and gone on into their seventies. But Delmore could see his life filled with other things.

He introduced himself to the group and then listened to the others. He was shocked by the appearance of some of them—clean cut white collar types especially—but it was what they said that got to him. They were self-pitying, self-centred, pathetic souls, the lot of them. But he knew the lousy lives they described, and how it was their first step towards changing.

He had to distance himself from old friends. And he really missed the early days of it, when his life seemed more exciting; a time of highs when the lurid stars brought him into their fold for nights of fighting and lust. But he wanted to walk along the beach with Marisa, the ocean beside them still loud and yet far away. He wanted the realities of Marisa's world and all the things in it; wanted the poetry of her voice and her mind and her body and her hair and her smell and her clothes. He knew it would take all those things.

PICTURES FROM HOPPER

I . GAS

There he is; the thick trees in motion behind, the waiting road and the grasses to be blown. Can't just sit down, wait, always has to fiddle about with something. Look at him, immaculate in waistcoat and slacks, the taut, crisp sleeves of his snow-white shirt above his taut, white, working arms, the black tie like the black in the green of the trees. Look at his razored falling face, the eyes flatly downward, the cream on his neat parted hair, the legs close together for balance but not because of age. If you passed or stopped you might seem him moving around like the shadow that he is by the roadside, you wouldn't go inside, past the white painted wood that lights the outside.

There is the light, and there is the road, and there are the trees and their promise of darkness. But take your eye from there, beyond which the brook runs towards open spaces where the blue sky is filtered throughout with the glorious cumulus only hinted at above the treetops; where a farm sits among the growth of flowers and cows and the road is like a nick of grit in the moist eyes of a vision filled with skin. Go back then, to the artificial throw of light and the painted artifice of the station walls. Pass the pumps and set your shadow among the light. Trace your way with

17

fingers over the untouched spotless forecourt where his
feet barely make impressions though they re-trace the
same steps day after day, year after year, in breaths of
immaculate waiting. See then the three shining pumps
and the leaping logo up the post and with the branches;
see the road beyond the post, curving into the shade of
leaves of branches; see not that nobody comes or goes
now, see that I came from shade, stayed, only to go and
come back nightly from drinking and dancing and the
long sunsets of this state that fall slowly over the long
writhing grasses. Why is it that through sententious
struggles I keep coming back here to escort this old
man into the darkness of the trees? What of my story
in this crated wilderness, where the road leads away
both ways from the red painted pumps? It is here that
the story lies, not elsewhere in the limitless vistas, but
here in the tiny space our lives supply; in this stained
spot where we stay; this seemingly motionless pose that
waits for use and facilitates speed and movement. The
red of the pumps, and the red that reaches some way
up the post, and the red of the roof and the red hinted
at in the rustling undergrowth that moves upwards
towards the thickness of the trees: these are my reds;
the red of my blood dripped and rising; the red of my
lifeblood; the red of my frustrated face; the red of my
face rising above and beyond the writhing fields. The
whites are all his, from the colourless illuminated head,
to the angles of the kerbstones, to the slow falls away
to the road, to the white wood nailed precisely behind
which he lies in white, colourless, bloodless, under
sheets that hold him in and that he never forces loose.

Why is it that we live in such places when the life is
beyond and above the trees? Why do our fancies turn

to chopped and shaped wood? Why can't I do it, why can't I be brave, why must I wait for the shining curves of a Chevrolet filled with drunks? Beyond the trees in the brook, I've been swimming with the fishes, have laid down on the polished stones to let the clarity of the water flow over my starlit frame and thrill my organs into being, I've been dripping with sweat and water and love but still. I've been down in town to taste Coca Cola and ice cream and sit with my shivering legs in the sun; I've taken cheap books and wasted the sunlight hours searching for cowboys and their guns. And I've seen those guns, believe me, plenty of them, and dreamed of a single shot ringing and sending life shooting from the branches into blue. I've dreamed of it so often on constricted nights imprisoned with starch, listening hour after hour, lulled by the occasions of sporadic breath.

See this same scene as the darkness approaches and the three circles shine even brighter, see the trees just a black ridge of mountains beneath the deepening blue to black of the sky, see the light thrown off from inside, a quick fade and the joining up of black, see the man reduced to the whiteness of his shirtsleeves; see those shirtsleeves hollow, blown around on a flagpole, see a Chevrolet, filled with gas, tail lights gone under the eaves of trees, see an empty cash register hanging open, see a man on the floor with his head like hacked ice, see the folded up flag of the American dream in a polished dresser draw, in the tiny corner of a bedroom; see me gone, see me going, see me with hair thrown back from the window; see another town; see another man, see another filling station—maybe an Esso one, or maybe another Mobil one — see nothing at all until the new morning of blue skies and vistas and light.

2. SECOND STORY SUNLIGHT

She was so sweet. Can you believe she didn't like her body and yet would kiss, night after night, my sunken, usually, drunken, frame? I'm probably reading her the Bishop poems of which we were so fond. I liked 'The Moose' and she liked 'Chemin De Fer' and 'In the Waiting Room', and, well, I don't remember exactly, though it's likely, but let's say that morning I was driving her along through the patient precisions of Bishop. You see her arms? Almost like a man's. But her soft body and her sweet sensibilities and her sharing delicate touches took her away from the vulgar realms of any men I'd ever known.

When they landed on you and then rolled off and started into snoring, well, that was men to me. And in the morning when they wouldn't want to talk about it — or talk about anything at all — I'd lie there looking for something in the sated vacancies of their eyes. Even the man I had a child with sank with failure like a broken board in the surf, and that was before I left him, maybe even why I left him. But with Emmy and the women before her I found what was missing: their delicate touches and our illicit coupling and their kisses and cleanness and tenderness, and their bodies. At first it was bodies like my own, youthfully wasted by men, left loosened with age but loved by the tender touches of contemporaries. And then there she was. On the street. Make-up smudged and baleful, the yellow cabs glistening with neon and streetlight left faded by her blonde and brazen and youthful beauty. She came with me to the subway and then we walked the silent street to my third-story walk up, my ears pricked and my body shaking to the sound of her heels that clacked and scraped on the pavement then the stairs. And in a night almost above and beyond accurate remembrance, and certainly not possible to recreate with written words, we drank between us the second best thrills of gin, and with what must have been intuitive skill she sat between me with her mouth and sent me to a twitching and shivering I'd never even come close to before, my hands running through her blonde tresses, clutching at her white skin, my hand over my own mouth in habitual shame and new surprise. Even now with her gone it thrills me. But I have my pictures and memories and the second story sunlight by the sea, where she sits looking away from me and down at the sands. It takes me to my view then, of the sea and the sky and on the left the moistening sensation of her profiled breasts, the sparkle of the sun on the sea reduced to repose, the acreage of her white thighs in sunlight and her scratched and bitten calves in the shade. And in my face you can see the wistful remonstrance of my thoughts, the fragmented, clouded, drink tinged fingers of memory. All that wasted youth I urged her not to copy. And in my prophetic and self-destructive giving she saw some sense and a future, so that she looked out to sea and went there, leaving me in second story sunlight, my once ascendant career and my life slowly drawing down like the yellowing shades you see behind us in the long windows. The wind through the trees that you can see ready to move her flaxen, dull gold hair is the same wind I'm pinned back against. And I still read Bishop on the balcony in the mornings as the sea moves forward and back in the ceaseless interchange of the seasons, and still I have my pictures. And still I have my Emmy. And still I have the laughter of discovery, the thrilling memory of moisture, the first night and all the other nights and days we spent together in the month or two that now seems to be the largest constituency of my life.

I can't tell you too much about the rest of her time. Much of that truth has been lost in the news-papers — newspapers that, for a start, never knew about me. And they would never know the morning I picked up their papers and saw time and again in black and white the same picture of the snow-surrounded wreckage. And how that morning I went out onto the balcony and screamed at the sands and the sea. And how I went down to the shore intent on swimming and swimming and came back and collapsed on the sand without the faintest idea why.

For weeks I saw his picture in the paper and for weeks I read of his grief, and the reports that said the nation's hearts were going out to him in his time of need. I watched without bitterness how he threw himself into his work and his career and with the backing of an empathetic public reached award-winning heights. I saw him marry again, another beautiful blonde much younger than him, older than Emmy ever reached.

Sometimes looking out at the surf I see her in the youthful bodies of blondes. I see her as they shake their locks from bathing caps and collapse panting onto towels placed for them on the sands. I see her drying herself, her chest in falling and rising refrain. I see the droplets of ocean on her pinking thighs. I think of all the times we rushed back from the beach for cocktails. But now it's every morning warm enough to swim that I see her though not myself on the balcony in the second story sunlight. The alabaster of her skin. My fingers pressing through it. The blue of her costume. The imminent movement of her hair. The imminent movement away. I wonder, did she ever think of me as she smiled for the cameras in those captured moments of mortal youth and beauty?

3. THE LIGHTHOUSE AT TWO LIGHTS

When, as a child, we went to live under the twirling lights of the lighthouse at two lights, it was those twirling lights that moved over the darkness that preserved the visions of what happened in my memory. So for me it seems that the light sent flashing into the skies and air above the waves is a beacon not so much for boats and ships but the boats and ships crossing to this shore from the past, complete with all the swells and blindness and sickness and salt smells and rope.

My own must also see the light as it swirls through the trembling curtains across us, and I know not what memory of childhood will go forth again from here. My own hope is that memories of love will move with them through time; memories of love and, I hope, forgiveness, and that, should they read this, they might once more come and see me before I succumb to the routine of different lights.

Some days I'd hide in the shaking bushes stuck on

the down slope of the grassed over rocks that ran down to the immensities of the blowing and rolling feathers of the waves. Out of the full force of the wind I'd hold my legs to myself and squeeze my blood together and sit looking at the sea through the cover of bushes to let the cleaning comforts sedate me. Sometimes I'd sit there and watch the sun go down and flatten on the horizon, squashed and spreading out only to die in an immeasurable pinkness. Sometimes it would deepen in orange so that it was the colour itself that made the sunburst and go, and best of all, most apposite or so it seemed, were the early sunsets of September and October, when the sun would go as red as the red circle on the Japanese flag, then split as though startled into a bloodshot stream of decline.

On summer nights I'd sneak out and try to jump into the gleam of the beams; the beams of light sent out onto the sea, only to stumble and fall backwards towards oblivion. I'd look at that sea: all black at night beside the beams; a blackness touched on and passed over.

In the shadows cast by the angles of the whitewashed walls, you could see where the wind and rain had taken the paint away, so that the shadows themselves seemed deepened, and when you looked from the turrets of the lighthouse steps you might turn your eye from the sights of the rooftops; rooftops you might lose faith in when the weather turned to its worst.

At the bottom of the lighthouse you could open the door onto an oblong of wave, and it was to here that supplies were sometimes made. I'd watch from behind as it went on, and the things that kept us going in our fashion were passed hand to hand over the lee between the boat and the lighthouse. When climbing up the ninety eight stairs from there, past the turrets that showed the shadows cast by the angles of the white washed walls and the fragilities of the enduring rooftops, I'd get out of breath and excited at the same time and wouldn't feel the sadness that accompanied other moments of breathlessness. Sometimes, different nights, my shadow visible to mariners, I'd be party to a remorse they'd never catch among the waves.

One day a fat, ornate gull came and sat its shaking whiteness out by one of the bushes. It looked about nervously and left a quick drooling of white behind on the slope, before labouring off up and away.

Nowadays nobody mans the lighthouse, and the lights come on and off at prescribed, automated times in tune with the annual moments. When rare accidents happen there's nobody to see, just those directly involved with the fathoms, battling with the wind and rain on the darkness of winter nights where the light that shines can do nothing to assuage damage already done. And always and forever standing above them will be the lighthouse, where no heart lies beating inside, where no feet walk the descending circles down and where the whole conical edifice that rises upward remains emptied and unreplenished.

From where I am now I can't shake the picture and it's a picture I seem to have repainted. It hangs, framed, on the wall in front of me, only thanks to the good grace of those that decide on such things. But I wonder if it correlates at all with the picture in my mind, and if it does or it docsn't, what that has to do with the diffusion of angles in twirling light. For it might be that it's only in my mind that the damage is done in the dark corners, and I don't really know how many steps are in the lighthouse or if its automated at all, or even if any ships and boats go past there periled or otherwise. I can only part way convey what my picture is and what the painted picture shows, so you need some access to colour yourself and only you can decide if it's important to you to know how and why its painted.

For me it seems the painting and the pictures go on and sometimes there's more of me in them than in others. For example, not all of you might know what my legs are like, but I know how all of you can picture them, and though all of you can guess at my past, not all of you will get at what it is I've been able to convey and what I haven't, and it's for you to decide what is and what might be my fate, if I'm devil or angel or some parts of both and how much. And when I say 'all of you' there is no absence of irony; just know that irony isn't all.

4. OFFICE AT NIGHT

That was a dress, let me tell you. And that was Mr Ames, right there; Mr Ames, under his little desk, with his little telephone and lamp. I'll tell you how I remember it, shall I?

Miss Fires, he said. That's a nice name, he said, and on the first day he said it again. I sat down on the desk opposite. He could see my legs and I saw his slim pant legs and little shiny shoes. I crossed and uncrossed my legs with little nylon rustles all that first day and onwards and soon enough he had me staying later. But he kept the door open and the big lights on as well as the lamp, and so the light from street lamps washed into the already well-lit room. Like a fool he kept the drape open, so that anyone on the road could look in passing.

Mr Ames, I said, won't you close the drape? I'm awful tired of people gawking in.

I need the air, Miss Fires, he said. It's too hot in here already, he said, looking at every inch of my dress.

I think you should, Mr Ames. Let me do it for you Mr Ames, I said, and he demurred and I brushed past him and stretched up and pulled down the drape.

So at last that was a signal that he was finally brave enough and, in a rush, he turned off all the lights and closed the door. I could see the sweat on his face. He brought my chair over and put it next to his. Then he took off my heels and stroked my feet and kissed them and I did up the top button on the dress. Within a few minutes of the drape closing, Clyde had come in and cracked Mr Ames over the head with the gun. We tied him to the chair and knotted one of his own cotton socks around his mouth and Clyde was fine; looked so fine, and he said, hell, Mary Fires, show me that safe, and I did and fished out the key from my dress and he opened the safe and it looked like all our life was there in that bundle of green. I was so excited, let me tell you. I knew that that was what a man should be and I felt it all everywhere and how Clyde looked so fine, and we walked out of there so calm, but I wanted to scream out loud and all down them quiet streets; scream at all those church going people.

And when Clyde moved us away just as calm as could be I put my hand on his thigh and when we got to the end of Main Street I said, *Hit it!* And he did, and we streaked away between the cornfields as the evening sky went black. We were listening to the radio for reports but nothing came on except music, and when Benny Goodman started playing, Clyde just swerved us off the road and right into the cornfields, and with the moon and stars shining down the skyline of mountains we danced in a flattened hideout, kissing as we counted the money.

Mr Ames had his day in the courthouse, but we'd made the papers. Some of those folks in the gallery were rooting for us, I know that. Most folks are happy to work all their days and go to church on Sunday and thank the lord for their blessings, but wouldn't you once just like to drive out of town with a good looking outlaw like Clyde, a bagful of dollars on your lap, the wind blowing across you and through your hair as you sped away from your boring life? Well, I'll tell you, I worked in that office, day after day, trying to be like a good old girl, the kind of girl my mamma always wanted me to be, and I'll tell you I was dying; dying inside every day; dying every time I stepped inside that office. That Mr Ames, hell, he was scared of me and I guess that means he was scared of life. I know that dress wasn't the finest, but you know how Clyde looked at me in it, you know that feeling don't you? Tell me that you do. And don't talk to me about 'objectifying'. First thing I bought with some of the bundle of green was a mighty fine red number and when I showed it to Clyde he kind of set to howling like a wolf and I knew right there he'd kill for me if he had to, and when they got to us at the crossroads he did, and when Clyde jumped out to firing I tell you he looked so fine, and when they hit him he kept trying to get up, but it took ten men to kill Clyde, and in the end he was lying in the blood and dust by the highway, his white hat rolling off of its own volition like some small part of him was still trying to be free.

And I couldn't have told you then I'd be drinking cocktails on the lawn with the chief of police, but I didn't know when I was with Clyde that sometimes those on the side of the law can be exciting too, and break the laws they are supposed to uphold with sometimes the same abandon as outlaws. I can tell you, it's not the same as with Clyde, but it's kind of the same but different if you can understand me now. Hell, you got to find something in this life that gets your blood up. How come, in the whole history of the place, with all the things we can do, why do so many of us spend our days in offices? Why in the hell is that? If you ask me it's because there's too much of Mr Ames and not enough of Clyde in this world that's why.

5. HOTEL BY A RAILROAD

It's early morning and she sits pretending to read while her husband looks out of the window smoking. The decanter is empty, as are the rails. The mirror holds a reflection of the wall in morning sunlight. The armchair in which she sits blocks easy access to two of the drawers in the dresser. The green drape in the bedroom is half-raised. There is a thin black line in the split between the white curtains below it. He is standing before her, looking out of the window and over towards the right. He has some hair remaining, combed neatly beneath his bald pate. He holds what is left of a cigarette in his upraised right hand. She is waiting for him to speak. He is poised. She has long grey hair and a body untouched by children. The expression on her face is one of shame; but shame on the surface of other things.

She is me, and that is a morning I won't forget. It is a morning singular in terms of the occurrences preceding it, and the changes wrought in me forever after. For you see, he was even older than I was.

When we first met he was a relief—a mature, listening relief—but the peak of other things was a long time gone for him and something coming in a silent rush for me, so the protective arms—that once led to soothing and expert slowness—soon slept around me as I lay there listening to my breathing over his.

The hotel by the railroad was our home, and it fit my life as though the tracks going by were the memories of moving youth and the hotel itself the stable stopping off point of maturity. He owned it like he owned other things in town and he owned it like he came to own me, so that when I felt like taking my hands from what was left of his dead hair, I just sat by the window and watched the faces in the train windows, some of which looked back, most of which were talking to the face opposite, still others just looking ahead in limitless differences of blank and buffeted repose.

So what can one say of the spectre of youth in the middle years of it forever gone away? It is to say that I was beautiful beyond what you might imagine, and everything came to me, morning and night, in a pattern of proffered flowers. It was for me to choose which of the flowers to take and why I grew old with a vase full of different ones, where the smells still lingered and the fading colours could still be retouched by the golden light of whisky, the shaking comfort of cigarettes.

I had such power over them when my eyes were bright and my hair was shining and the skin on my face and all over my body was painted in depthless glamour. To those outside the room they held all the power, but when they came in with a saloon on their lips, all hard and begging to be sated, it was I who held the cards under the covers and in my waiting, wanting eyes. Don't misunderstand me, even in my beauty I was never one of those women that can be told, but I thought it was in my interests to sometimes seem that way, to give them the notion of power and make them feel like they had it always, but I can see now that that was because I wanted them all to be more than they could be, and without exception they failed.

Thinking back now, with the flowers in my hands, I know I couldn't handle those choices. Most of all of them had something the other didn't have and vice versa and, in short, I wanted to be the lover and not the beloved. That is why in mistaken and faded marriage I looked at little more than boys who came to the hotel. I saw the girls they wasted themselves with, wanted those boys for myself. I wanted my ageing body next to the shining, perspiring youth of theirs, their flat stomachs and perpetual readiness. I wanted a full head of shining, colourful hair through which I could run my hands and somehow take the wrinkles from my fingers. And I found it, one jewelled afternoon where no trains passed, and the sunlight shone against the drape, and his head moved among the pinstripes of light surrounding and my fingernails sank into his careless laughter, and I bit him through the difficulty of breathing.

But as is the wont of the beloved he got on the morning train, and I watched him with his fragrant, apparently useless beau of the moment: the gentlemanly lift as he hoisted her into his arms at the top of the steps, the bright faces of both, the seemingly guileless eyes and his golden ability. I watched to see for so much as a glance up to where he knew I was standing, but I watched his movement along the window glass, saw him sit by the window still smiling at her, and her just stupid and smiling back. And it was then that I sat and opened the book and smelt the cigarette and heard the shuffling walk.

In a moment the cigarette will be thrown through the window into sunlight. The book will be taken from her hands and thrown to the floor. Her arms will be gripped and her whole body will be shaken side to side. He will slap her face and pull her hair and throw her clothes from the wardrobe and into the suitcase on the floor. He will say nothing. She will say nothing. She will get on the train. She will reach another town, another room. She will have a future.

PICTURES FROM HOPPER #2

She is in summertime. She leaves the building, the opened window, the blowing curtains fanning freshening air into the salted room. The sheer shift of thigh beneath the feathered white. The hat that was jaunty yesterday above a pensive face, and eyes taken by the roughness, the emptiness, the removal of a flowered future. One hand rests on the supporting pillar, her red hair shines in the morning sun before the shadow of her elegance on the steps. The right leg leading down to the delicate black shoe is about to step off those steps. For you, standing across the road, having left your solitary room to step blinking into the sunlight of morning, she is all your soul wants to complete its genius. Her pale skin and tender, just-bruised youth, her hair, her painted lips, the eyes you can't trace, the mannequin-like stuckness of her expression, she is the cloud of fantasy that walks your gripped night, the moaning vision whose thigh you could span in a bound. You want to hold her, capture her glamour in the folds of your rushed imaginings. But you don't really want to approach her, because your life and what power you hold in it has been shaped by an absence of charms. You don't want to take beauty away with speech (yours and/or hers); you want her, painted forever in the morning, a model of a dream loved only by your mind. But despite yourself and

33

because of your life you run across the street to see her distracted face flicker briefly with alarm, then take you in, in a way you can't yet yourself. You speak but she doesn't listen. Don't you know that her life is real? That she's just walked from a room where all life was held and that your fancies are all of a delusion? But your solitary heart that you know is so big and so just waiting to give love blinds your eyes to what she wants and needs at this particular moment, and in your blindness you've lost everything to her black eyes, veterans of impression. So go back to your room and learn from your mistake, see with smiling eyes that summertime is yearly and beauty walks the ten-a-penny streets commonplace as a cloudscape. Move from your room and surround yourself with garlands, trace their lives with your listening ears, their bodies with your listening fingers, move from the squalid abstractions of poesy, prickle like imperfect legs, walk through sunlight and shadow, leave the plans in your own salted room, paint not bitter pictures but paint not perfections either, pause over the slipped and stiff-ened brush, the crashed canvas, the dried tubes; mix colours and stroke together, walk less alone into and out of all the blackened doorways, kiss their steps, lick concrete in the cravings of your life.

II

You sit in a cinema alone, waiting for the film. Around you the blue walls are ageing. Your black dress matches the empty black chairs around you. You stare with black eyes at a space below the stage, the curtains, the screen. There is an exit to your left, a tiny knob on the door. Your brownish hair is scraped back in a vision of practicality. The ankles above your black shoes, and the shins above them, have been untouched for as long as you remember. You think of the doctor.

The chairs around you wait for people to come back. Your shoulders cannot relax. In your repose you think of the chair next to you, the chairs behind you, the very edge of the chair across the aisle. The drab carpet in the aisle is the worn history of passage. There are no ice creams for sale.

The curtains pull back. You are washed in the light of cinema. You raise your head to look up. Your ankles relax. The chairs fill up all around you. An ice cream appears, ten foot tall. You fall in love with a giant face, giant eyes, giant, soulful eyes of experience, the eyes of a man 5'7". You melt in the scripted moments.

You leave the cinema. There is no queue on the way out. The white washed streets are filled with faces. Vivid movement thrills you. You are dispatched, detached. The heels of your shoes make no sound on the streets. Pigeon's rise cuts the sky. Rain comes in silver, glitters on your loosened shoulders, flattens the dress to a cling. You look up so that the rain falls on your face. Soon your hair is darkened, given sheen. You run your hands through it, shake it so it drips, throws out spray. Someone across the street stares at your revery, their eyes take you all in, bring you back to yourself. You fold your arms. The eyes leave you to look elsewhere. You are left with only your own eyes once more, once more looking only at yourself. Your ankles begin to feel cold, swell. You wish for a coat; buttons, pockets, cover. Your shoes slip slide and ruin your stride. You make your way under cover. You think only of yourself and getting home. You look at your feet, not at the pattern of fall around them. The silver rain is setting a shine on everything it wets, its substance sets movement to roaring, there is a wind-shifted movement of black among white and grey with touches of blue. Beside you someone stands with a broken umbrella, for years you have been the fixer of umbrellas. You are cold, your hair is wet, your ankles are swollen, the film is gone, you say nothing. A stranger walks into the rain swinging a broken umbrella. Everything in every moment is changing, and all is the same as it was.

III

You sit over your coffee. The hand holding the cup is lit, the other hand is in shade. The downward curves of your hat brim frame your porcelain, rouged face. The fruits are all in a bowl behind you, waiting for you to turn. Your legs are folded beneath the turquoise pool of the table. The chair that faces you is black and empty. The fur lining of the jacket you wear warms your frigid shoulders and wrists. You are in a recurring thought, a thought that time and again you forget until reminded.

Your beauty is half-existent in your own eyes. Others create it, and then become bored. Sometimes you think that if you don't speak at all then everything will be okay. When you do speak you think that you can't help but detract from perception. You see it in the glazing eyes that itch for the speech of superior thoughts. You are more than the fur trim, though you wear the fur trim. Your expanses are only ever warmed by golden radiators. Though you mispronounce the surnames of the French, and schooling was a battle with those envious of unwitting surface, the insensitive brushes of the smiling have painted your heart in unlimited colour.

At this moment you know that what you are waiting for will not come. Not yet, at least. As you age your pert breasts ache to give and sag and your womb is a boarded room. One day you will be able to give away the rose of yourself content of consequence and see the reflection in florid embers. Your thinning chest will plump and colour and warm for the suck of love. Within walls however small you will at last be able to escape the limits of perfection.

But, as you wait for the latest in a series of scenarios that change only in terms of smiles, you are too close to the pain of self pity, and will rise for speech and company too soon to think of changes. Many more solitary coffees await you in public spaces, but one day you will be brave enough to face the solitary coffees in your home, and you will have the time to think, and you will find a way to be alone without fear, to listen to the silences, to examine, to evaluate, and the pattern will emerge quicker than you might imagine, and you will see through the tresses of your fear, your whole body wrinkling in the wind until you come to the calm, and in that wrinkled repose you will look at the frames arrayed across the walls, and take a strand of your grey hair and place it into your own mouth, and die as beautiful as you were born.

Naked, smoking, you stand on a golden slab of sunlight, looking out through an open window at the memory of a moving car. Your athletic thighs useless, fixed, statuesque pillars of your frozen pose. The unmade bed and the absence of other furniture around seems a clue to departure. As are the sunlight split curves outside the window to your right, under a blue sky that seems to hold reflections of notes in green. Your golden naked-ness before the window is a rueful rather than defiant display. Above the songs of your thighs, the give of buttock, the softness of slim belly, the unevenness of your cherry cake breasts beneath the tautness of your bright jaw. There is a blue green to your eye, a coun-terpoint to the sky. Your eye holds more, as does the greying gold of your hair.

The large portrait behind you is rendered a blank canvas, the smaller frame before you an irrelevant store-bought platitude. Your new black shoes will seem some kind of solace in days ahead, when you will lie on the bed and hold them before your eyes, fondle them, feel their curves of black. You will push the heel into your naked thigh until your naked thigh bruises a dot of blue. You will sense a softening of your heels.

You try to recall words; words you'd taken for true. You realize the words were meant to make you feel that way, give access to the yellow gold of your ath-letic, practised frame for sheet changing nights of con-solation on a narrow bed where you intertwined in heat and sweat and a morning kind of condensation. You see now that you were just another moment in the life of someone else's youth, a stopping point for their adventures in skin, just another justifiable reason for the increased pleasures of the rest. But what of you, left behind, smoking? Are you to lie back on the bed and run your hands through your golden grey hair? Look at those worked hands and see wisps of silver grey through the fingers?

The slab grey surfaces of your future seem to slide flatly towards death. But on a new morning, when the fields and sky might as well be grey as any other colour, you will get dressed because you have to and put your softened heels into the lingering beauty of your black shoes. You will sit on the bed and brush your hair and watch dust fall to the dusty floor. You will step out onto the street and keep walking. Your brain and your beauty will return you time and again to short lived approximations of your search, and in your moments alone you will see them in moments of rapture, their faces in clouded glow, and the speed of their resurgent departure as they speed on, as yet unknowing of their future and their memory of you; a memory that, on certain days, will take them to bars, for they will need something more than selfish flesh and bone to take away your kindness, your particular scent, the moonlit visions of your giving body, the haunting refrain of your nurturing, amazing whisper.

V

The whole room is a possibility, and the angles of light fall in differing shades of gold. The window shows the side of a tree in the breeze, sun on the leaves and the darkened shade beneath. The wall around the

39

window shows some reflection of that green in both light and memory. The angle of the sunlight would suggest the height of the day, and that the quietness is attributable to work. There is still some psychology in the corner, but the sunlight is a passage from the frame into the air that more fully contains it. Today, someone is moving *in*.

PICTURES FROM HOPPER #3

In the touching fall of sunlight the barn on the hillside was given a sybaritic mark that stuck on the souls of the boys. The distant houses in the shadow of sandy hills had been their home since they'd had to move, and under the red roof and whitewashed walls they were taught courtesy and manners and morals, as well as history, composition, geography, Latin, science. In the evenings, in the shadow of the sandy hills, they threw a softball between them, its swerving curve of white vivid under the clear, wind-stroked, drifting down sky. When at last they got a shaped stick of hickory, they oiled it like the instructions said, smelled it in waiting, and then, when it was dry, swung at the surrounding fresh air. Under arm pitches gave them practice, and finally Joe connected in a poetry of timing, barely feeling the ball on the swinging bat and watching with blinking eyes as it rose in a sunset washed arc, far up and away, before landing with a soundless bounce on sand halfway up one of the welcoming hills. John ran after it laughing, stumbling, before picking it up and holding it aloft like a first fish, and from where Joe stood, in a rapture of promise, the ball looked tiny, vanquished, stitched with damage as much as precision. When John came back begging for the bat, it was passed from one boy to the other like a weightless tablet. When Joe's adrenalin packed pitch whistled towards John's head and dumped him on the sandy grass next to the bouncing bat, John got up and ran over to his brother, and they kicked and punched and scratched themselves towards darkness and the point of exhaustion.

Mark O'Malley, the club professional, watched with intense, life draining boredom as the old couple he was coaching whacked and sliced and hooked and fluffed and bickered their way around the course. The polish and glint of the silver shaft and the elegant crafting of the club heads was rendered irrelevant by the O'Hara's, who might as well have been bashing at the dimpled balls with hammers and mallets. As the darkness approached, and O'Malley could taste the tang of lemon in his first longed for gin and tonic of the evening, the O'Hara's both hit their approaches into the bunker before the eighteenth green. A full half hour later, sand scattered across his sun reddened face from their continual slashing and hacking, O'Malley smiled and waved them on their cantankerous way, before raking the bunker and wandering with increasing speed to the welcoming bar of the clubhouse.

Mary Bardsley waited, poised and apparently aloof before the glinting array of glasses. Berets often partly covered her blonde hair, other times that blondness was set off with a gardenia or a simple lily, an allusion to some lost purity. On this evening her blonde hair was held back by a white band so that the oval deceptions of her face shone across the very length of the bar. She added ice and a slice of lemon to the gin and tonic, and without any exchange of commonplaces put the glass down.

'Mary, Mary, you are shaped in a vision of comeliness this evening, and would taste, I'm sure, like gin itself to these dry lips,' O'Malley said. 'What brings you to this deserted cove of lost souls this mournful evening?'

'You've been out in the sun too long,' she said, smiling, drying washed glasses casually.

'So tell me something I don't already know,' he said, looking in the mirror at the tan line on his forehead where his cap had only partially protected him. 'Your blonde visions come in poetry to my Irish, sing-songing soul.'

As the drink cooled and then revived him, O'Malley thought of his big empty house by the railroad. 'Why don't you come home with me tonight?' he asked Mary.

'I think that sun did get to you.'

'No really, let me take my time with another of these and then I'll drive us.'

On the coast highway the smell of sea breezes mixed with gasoline and blown dust. The opened windows of O'Malley's car were a necessity in the humid night, despite their altitude moving up and over the hills. Beginning their descent towards O'Malley's, they saw the lights and heard the comforting rumble of a passing freight reaching through the darkness. O'Malley looked down at Mary's white shirt blowing, her manicured hands covering her modesty in accustomed and gentle press.

As the parked car tilted forward, Mary looked up at the majesty of the house. O'Malley's departed parents, having given less than everything of themselves to him in life, partly compensated him in death, the rising

43

woodcut grandness of their bestowal a testament to their work ethic and resultant relative prosperity.

It stood then, in the morning overlooking the rails, rising up to the skies, a portent of designated grace, the pillars of the entrance way like the ageing pins of a society belle. Its neglected exterior shone in the silver blue of the morning, and the weak rising of the sun at the side cast other windows in shade and shadow. The window shade in their room was half lifted to let in that sun, though not too much for eyes reflecting the morning sorrows of whisky and gin. O'Malley washed and shaved, whistling and singing, content and complacent.

'Mary, Mary, quite contrary, how does your garden grow,' he said, laughing to himself, not even looking at her wasted eyes, her lifeless body. 'Let me drive you home this morning.'

As he made himself some breakfast, Mary dressed and put on her sunglasses before lighting a cigarette. She looked under the half lifted window shade, the blackened light on the still fields and the small hills weaving in and out between stalks of grass that seemed to flicker in some fear. She raised the window shade entirely and as the noise of the engine heightened she watched its steady procession along the tracks, its curve towards town, sleepers spurting out in horizontal equanimity behind.

In the car she felt the dread of another day at the club, and couldn't help but listen as O'Malley waffled on about his eight iron. His too obvious happiness detracted every minute from the minutes of half reached revery lost too quickly the night before, when gin had at last relaxed her, showed her, in the big shadowy house, some bearable intimations of the future. And perhaps by the afternoon, when she'd cleaned up and maybe slept some, the absence of deep feeling might be forgotten again in the affirming rodomontade.

She didn't watch O'Malley's car drive off. Dressing she put a yellow ribbon in her hair, a yellow dress on and went to the club. Through the windows of the bar she saw the sprinklers shimmer and the dropped stars on the manicured grass, heard the clock of club on ball, the sound of faint waves in the air, the gentle clatter of bags thrown over shoulders, gentle laughter, gentle banter, all the sustaining gentilities of membership. She was glad when the first of them, the earliest of them, returned; was glad to indulge the flirtations of the moneyed old boys and to take their generous tips in return. She liked the way they looked at her; liked that sense more than the experienced actualities, and the afternoon moved into the evening with all the inevitability of silver.

O'Malley had Mrs Farrel's hands on the shaft, showing her the advantages of backspin. In the light of the night before he enjoyed the holes with her, and was showing her his swing. He was moving around behind her, ready to illustrate the ideal head position when for some inexplicable reason she swung the club round and cracked him clean on the forehead. For a moment he rose and she had a shocking intimation. Then he fell flat on his back and sank, one of his dead hands flopping on her untouched tee so that the small ridge of plastic emerged between his fingers. She wailed 'Fore!' and a dozen old men on the course looked around and covered their heads. She saw her bag of clubs, and the clubhouse on the horizon, and wailed again until Chill Wills and Strother Martin crossed over from the fourteenth.

'Well, he wasn't the best pro this club has ever had,' said Chill, as Strother nodded in agreement and Mrs Farrel collapsed in apoplexy. Chill picked her up, and Strother lifted her bag, and when they went back to the clubhouse and told Mary the story of what had happened she went into the store room ready to cry and laughed instead, so uproariously that the tears came that way. Mrs Farrel sat shaking on a bar stool, drinking brandy and waiting for her husband to be excused from work. By the time he arrived to put his arm around her, she was in a glassy eyed state that he remembered with a fondness from the early days of their marriage. But really she was failing to hide disappointment. Harold Farrel got himself a drink and another one for his wife, and consoled her while smoking a large cigar.

O'Malley hadn't made a will, and the house by the railroad was left to further decay, so that if you were to pass on a train and look up at it, you might think it a decaying shambles and expect it to fall in a collapse of dust caused only by the vibrating of the rails.

For Mary the whole town began to hold memories the vividness of which she wished to reduce, so like before she moved away, took the train to another town to re-invent herself again in a country so big you could be anything to anybody as long as you gave the past to someone else. From the window of the train she saw the house in which she'd made a kind of love with a man who no longer breathed, and she thought the whole edifice on the verge of collapse. As she moved away she saw for the last time too the distant designs of the golf course, the bunkers like spots of sand, the tiny flags like those on a baby's cake, the green pathways of the fairways and the moving to wildness of the semi rough and rough, the geriatric slowness's and the odd glint of swinging silver between trees.

Emerging from sleep she saw small water towers and a billboard with a big pair of staring eyes. She panicked briefly then felt for and looked at her ticket. How would she be in this town? Could she invent a plausible past that would put the new providers of her comfort at ease, help the real truth of moments gone by drift away like realities in a horizontal haze of drink?

Mary sat waiting in the hotel lobby in a blue dress that showed the pertness of her body. Her pale legs were stretched out and crossed, the many-miled calves gently bulging above small feet in green strap on shoes with small heels. She was reading through the train timetable, looking for locations with the loose and fluid criterion of a poet. If the names seemed to suggest something to her she remembered them, while others fell to the past like splashes between stations.

Standing before her was Lanton Mills, a refined old man once of 6'3", with a silver bush of moustache and the upright trained posture of a cavalry captain that was really caused by a bad back. He had his brown overcoat draped over his right arm, and with his right hand was gesturing for his wife to lead the way out. She sat back in a chair, her black fur coat unbuttoned revealing a faded red dress, the coat set off by her black hat, and the green peacock feather lolling back from the top of that hat matched in hue by Mary's green shoes and a strip of carpet that stretched in a green stripe to the door.

Mary kept scanning the listed names and the times of arrival and departure, but couldn't help overhearing the Mills':

'It's quite the time to go now, Eudora,' said Lanton, still shooing his wife with his right hand.

'Well, I'm sorry, but I'm not going to the god blasted football game. I hate football, I always have. Takes too long and you can't even see those young boy's faces.'

'Eudora, you are a stubborn woman, and I'm not going to stand here in this lobby while Farnsworth pretends not to listen over there and this beautiful young lady tries to read,' he said, looking over at Mary, who waited a few moments before raising her head and smiling gently, in the way that had always beguiled men, at least until they got bored with it and found something more crooked for their debasements; and in a way that certainly beguiled Lanton; beguiled him so much that the very shape of her lips took him back to a woman he'd long forgotten, a cheerleader from his first season, a corn–fed angel deflowered in a rustle of pompoms. 'My dear, please forgive my wife. She was once as beautiful as you, but now she's old and tired and doesn't like football anymore.'

'Lanton, I've *never* liked football and after forty years I thought I might come to like *you* by now, but you're the same mule you always were, you're just an old mule, and god blast it! I have *never* liked football!' And with that she rose unsteadily to her feet, steadied herself and regained her composure. 'Excuse me my dear, but I am going back upstairs. Forgive us, for we know not

48

what we say,' and with that she made her way to the elevator.

'Well that settles it,' said Lanton. 'Mam, will you kindly accompany me to the football? I used to play for the *god blasted* team and, I'm sorry, but not everyone gets these seats. Will you come with me, mam, will you make an old man happy, keep him company?'

'Sure. What else have I got to do?' she answered. Then she asked him to wait while she went upstairs for her coat and he did so, and when she came back down he held the door open for her, and held her arm gently down the stairs, then opened the door of the cab too before telling the driver to take them to the stadium.

Lanton Mills had been a kicker. His slight limp both belied and confirmed his past, and his finest moment was the year when, with only seconds left on the clock, he won the national football league championship for his team with a field goal from seventeen yards. He'd played for 22 years, and the gift they gave to him on retirement was exactly what he'd asked them for: two seats high up above the halfway line. And it was there that he sat in the light from Mary's blonde hair, basking in the memory of all the blondes in his heyday, watching his beloved team; the team that defined his life not just in his own mind, but in the minds and the dewy eyes of a thousand and more old timers for whom his kicks had given both thrills and solace in their moments free from lumber yards and car plants, factories and fields. His face had been on billboards, he'd done commercials for everything from chewing gum to toe bandages, and his legacy was confirmed in street names and his inclusion in the all time list. Now, in the limelight of his post career life, he struggled to find

49

meaning in the everyday reading of the newspaper, mowing the lawn, sipping cocktails with friends, floating in the false glimmer of swimming pools. At night, in both dreams and waking, his head was filled with an all mixing range of remembered moments from his starred career. And watching the game was the nearest he could get to his defining glories, high up in the stadium among the smells of hotdogs and hamburgers and beer, and though Mary began to think herself a curse when she turned at the end of the third quarter to see him motionless and on the way to rigidity, she realized that she helped him die in the midst of a waking dream, among the sights and smells and triumphs of his life, with her, a blonde thirty years his junior.

After the funeral, where old timers lined the streets in a cortege that passed by the fields of his precocious and practising youth to the stadium and all around, long after headlines that ranged from respectful to elegiac to faintly comic, Eudora Mills had calmed down long enough to contact Mary Bardsley, knowing that the beautiful younger woman of whom at first she might have been jealous was simply the golden accompaniment to her husband's final moments. Eudora wondered at the loneliness of a beautiful woman who would spend an evening of her life with an old goal kicker, and decided to track her down.

She hired a private detective who found her in the room of another hotel, and Eudora phoned Mary to arrange a convenient meeting. Mary was puzzled but had come to see how her life was shaped and defined by others. And never having lived before, she didn't know if this had improved her life or stolen it from better moments beyond her own making.

Eudora had enlivened her dotage and escaped entire days and nights with her goal kicker husband through, with his help, the purchase of a convenience store, where she spent her days in the therapeutic stacking of shelves, looking out through the windows, and occasionally transacting a sale. But since Lanton passed away she had nobody she had to endure for whole days and nights. Now the whole country could be her refuge, and she planned to spend some of her last years in the aimless floating drift of pointless travel.

Paint me a rural convenience store then, an hour after dawn. See its sanitized stillness, waiting in the moments before Mary puts her key in the lock and changes it forever with the shadows of her gentle movement. See the sparse display as yet unchanged: three wine bottles, a solitary 78 with a solitary trumpeter on the cover, a calendar of the years' remaining months and days, the dusty till in repose, the elegant working clock on the wall, the imputation of 7 a.m. See to the other side of the door the half closed yellow window shade, about to be raised, see it raised, see the sun fill the room, see Mary wiping away dust with patient, meditative touch. See close by the dark green blowing trees about to be heard again from the store. See the window above the store, behind which Mary will lie in bed, listening to them blowing before sleep, waking to them, hearing their light inhabitants, listening to the total silence of days and nights without wind, birds.

After Nathan Brittles first walked in for beer he walked in every night. When she heard he had been a sports- man it seemed a commonplace pattern to her. But he hadn't been famous like Lanton, he was more like Mark O'Malley the golf pro, the kind of sportsman that makes up the majority in tenuous and fading purpose. As a young man of 6"8 he had been offered a basketball scholarship at a prestigious college, and had achieved a share of local celebrity and parochial legend as the spectacles wearing, slam dunking hero of auditorium triumph. But just as he was attracting attention from teams in the national league, he landed awkwardly after sinking a basket, twisting his knee on the sweat shiny floor and tearing ligaments beyond effective repair.

This could have been a lifelong source of bitter- ness for Nathan Brittles. But rather than bemoaning a gloried, light bulb popping career that may have only ever existed in his mind, he changed courses and trained to become a microbiologist. He spent his days examining microscopic samples, and his nights drink- ing beer and listening to 78's, sometimes entertain- ing female friends — many of whom would wake to the relaxing sight of Nathan in bed beside them, his huge feet sticking out over the end of the too small bed — but most often reposing alone, escaped in music.

He was an extraordinary sight that first time he ducked into the store for beer. All 6"8 of him in a loose fitting grey suit, the trousers of which ended just above his ankles, his big horn rimmed glasses covering half his face, the lenses so thick you might think he'd taken them off his microscopes. And after he picked up the six pack, the beer cans seemed lost in his hands. When he saw her he took off his glasses to make it seem he was taking a closer look, when in reality it was done for effect, the removal rendering all indistinct that didn't move.

The day he bought the solitary 78 as well as his six pack he asked Mary if she would like to come around and listen to it after she closed the shop. She knew of his reputation in the town but decided to ignore the evidence of rumour. She hesitated, after closing the shop, between the stairs up to the known quantities of her room and the waiting way out. But once she heard the trumpet she knew that nerves were what made her, and was ready again for that skip that fades the glare.

She could tell from just the way he was that he'd had many women, and that he also liked to spend time alone, and that he didn't need her, just wanted her. She guessed that he wasn't someone with whom she was going to have children or grow old with. But he *was* gentle and loving and sensitive, and the most unselfish lover she'd ever had, seeming to gain the most of his own satisfaction in the developing of hers. And she thought that the way nights with him gave colour to the days was enough, as much as she could ask for. It came as a great surprise when he went down on his one good knee and asked her to marry him.

The companionship that always seemed to come her way without her trying was put in place again. And though she couldn't be entirely certain of how things would turn out, she went with what came her way, no longer waiting for walls to stretch in lines of love; for the tied sheets of the skies twined to fall into red cornstalks.

Before and after their marriage, when the car was in working order, Nathan and Mary would go on long evening drives in Nathan's open top Oldsmobile, and she loved the feel of the wind blowing her blonde hair around and the consummate skill with which he drove them. On coastal roads beneath dusty tournefortia she felt the free winds and brushed rare grains of sand from her tingling face and chest.

From the passenger seat she laughed at his jokes and bounced around her seat in his rushing approach up the bleached rise to the crossing. A road sign to their left gave directions three other ways. Across the tracks dark branches set back seemed to loom over the line. Beyond them were houses painted brown and white. At the very moment they began to bump across the tracks they were hit by the coastal freight, which pushed them along the lines for some half a mile before finally the brakes brought a halt to the crumpled meshing. Nathan and Mary had broken every single bone in their bodies, the crashing of their skulls against the windshield the most salient breakages of all.

Quinncannon, the driver of the freight, was so distraught that he just couldn't work again and he was pensioned off by the railroad company, spending his final days slumped and oddly content in the falling shade of peaches.

It might be of some consolation for us to know that Mary's memories, in the few happy months she spent married to Nathan, before he drove them into the onrushing path of a freight train carrying a thousand tonnes that broke every bone in their bodies, were for the most part filled with moments from her life that resonated with pleasure. And the most enduring of all her memories had been made in the barn, when she'd first seen the vividness of her budding breasts in their expectance, when they'd all three first felt the immolating graces that come in the ways we smile at each other in the wonderings and wanderings of love; in that never fully reaching out from our aloneness.

See then for one second your immersion in the tremulous saving of beauty: limitless fields blowing in the falling sun, speckles of that sun covering everything in luminous suffusion; see your bodies an intertwining of giving skin coiled through the desperations of three a.m., kissing in the twisting folds of cream, sinking through skin into each, bewildered by states of bliss; see all of us as golden birds in repose, golden waiting, once again expanding, shining up into flight through the thousand varying lights of morning. For in this way will come the raptures, floating, flying above the river, highest in the movement of trees.

PICTURES FROM HOPPER #4

Western Motel is one of Hopper's more famous ones, though not as famous as *Nighthawks*, which I don't really like much at all. It's a bit over-rated, has become something of a cliché. They said Edward Hopper's paintings were a 'mythicization of the banal'. I have to go into the garage to do mine. Anyway, *Western Motel*. It was five years into my first marriage, when everything of love had turned to working for the children. I met someone at an artist's retreat in the western isles of Scotland; we spent the last few nights of the trip together walking along the coast, making love in a B&B and on a blanket in the open air to the sounds of waves and seagulls. I put my ring back on halfway down the motorway. We lived about 500 miles apart and sent each other disgusting emails. He drove five hours to see me. I booked the B&B. Safe to say we never made one of those B's. Now, *Western Motel*. Well, she doesn't look like me at all but the expression on her face is one I recognize. The car to me is phallic, almost seems to go right through her, but it's the expression on her face. It asks for understanding. The hand gripping the chair shows that she is prepared to be judged, her face says just don't do it so harshly. She is a woman in a red dress with a plunging neckline and sensible shoes. Her hair is scraped back. She is aware of what she has done wrong, but the red dress overrides all. The scenery beyond the car could be beautiful but is rendered meaningless by her circumstances. She knows she has nowhere else to go but home, and big things wait there. The red lipstick has had to be reapplied time after time. She is a woman of poetry, a woman of art, a woman of the natural world, a woman most of all of imagination, imagination that flows when supplied, dries when denied. She has had enough of buttoned up nicety, loves that too, but not in isolation. For so long she yearned for unshaven men, physical men, men who didn't need her just wanted her. And the *Western Motel* is a symbol of a weekend when I was, well, I was going to say brave. But bravery didn't really come into it as much as necessity. It's all there in her face. How did Edward Hopper know all that? Maybe he didn't, maybe he did, maybe it doesn't matter. I just love him for having painted it, and its there, in reproduction, in a frame above my fireplace. The man I met in my *Western Motel* drove away from it without me, and that didn't matter in the slightest. I was prepared for that, knew what I had to lose to gain. I just, you know . . . anyway she's asking that you don't judge her. You know like the way the newspapers do, the way work colleagues do, the way gossips do. Because I know in my case the conclusions you might draw from the bare facts would lead you to erroneousness so profound that you might not ever recover, would go to your grave the same fool you were all your life. But now I'm judging you. I don't want to do that. I don't even know you, wouldn't profess to make assumptions based on such limited acquaintance. And anyway, I didn't wear a red dress, I

wore a purple jumper with holes in it, jeans, and trainers. No perfume, no makeup. It was a kind of test.
And he came at me like a starved lion. That line makes
me laugh and tells a story. And I couldn't hold anything back, had never had to before and never wanted
to. And I saw her face on reception, the feigned disin-
terest not quite covering the light in her eyes.

I'm trying to write this. It could be so quiet here.
But car alarms keep going off. And next door, through
the thin wall, I can hear all the conversations. They are
young people, which I don't mind in itself, but they
are so palpably dumb, and they seem to have such con-
formity. They watch all the popular programmes on
TV, they seem to laugh in a kind of forced way at the
most banal attempts at humour. It's a laughter of desperation. Now I know what it is to be really desperate.
They are just fucking dumb and it really annoys me. I
try to paint, this morning I'm trying to write. Maybe
it's because it's a Saturday. Monday will be better,
when they all fuck off back to work. Now maybe I'm
being judgemental. And did I always swear like this?
But I think, in basic terms, do I ever make any noise
that disturbs them? Ever? And the answer must be no,
unless they can hear brushstrokes or tapped keys. So
when I'm trying to concentrate and they waffle on, all
the time, it really fucks me off. I really think that some
people just can't cope with silence, and that's their
tragedy, in some ways. It's only my opinion but silence
holds the truth, and that's what so many are afraid of.
You have to face it. I think Hopper knew that, but I
look at Hopper's pictures and think he knew lots of
things. And I think his wife thought he knew lots of
things too. Lucky cow. Erm, yes. Maybe they can hear

me at night. That's a good reason for it, a real reason. Not laughing at the evasive irony of television.

Okay well, that's enough of that. Next one. Oh wait, I need the toilet. Well, okay, I might as well talk about the Hopper over the toilet. I'll get the laptop . . . right. Okay so its behind me but its vivid in my mind. *Girlie Show.* Now, in the picture she is bored, old and bored. All made up and bored. Going through the routine, simulating a sexual performance. The pianist seems almost suicidal, a death mask hovering over the black and white keys. We see only the backs of the heads of the sad watching few, the sad few for whom she's justified. But it's like sex in a dead marriage; a half hearted attempt motivated by love when lust has gone riding half cock over the hills.

But really what it takes me back to is a job I had in a bar. Sunday afternoon strippers, followed by a comedian. What pitiful wankers they were in there, drinking and leering and smoking and sweating and then laughing, totally drunk, at the well timed fascist punch lines of a warm hearted and jovial idiot in a suit. And the way they looked at me when they wanted their drinks, how they all wanted to fuck me, those little losers, but could never look me in the eyes because they were looking at my tits too. What kind of life is that? Where you work all week and then drink away your free time, staring at a woman beyond her physical peak without any other career options other than shaking her tits for a leering sack of losers. Now Hopper's woman has a fabulous body. The women in the pub didn't have bodies like that. I was covered up in comparison but looked way better underneath. And when they came for the money off the landlord I could have kissed them. But you couldn't talk to them; they had glazed eyes too far down a line of experience.

I used to look after my nails then; grew them long so they started curling under, painted them in patterns of stars and stripes. One day a man at the bar said they turned him on more than any naked woman ever could. I saw wisdom in those words, less wisdom in his degenerating presence.

What is it that makes a man get drunk? Well, I think it's all the clichés, because clichés start in truth and the subtleties of meaning get lost in over-familiar semantics. In short, its weakness, and you can put any slant on it you want, but its weakness. I knew a man who was thrilling with drink, but he was the exception, for he drank to rid himself of shyness and shyness isn't always linked with fear. Often its wisdom and knowledge that makes a man shy and the same qualities in the hands of the right woman can take him to a dukedom. But again, I digress. It's the way I think you see, concentrated but fluid. So, weakness, yes. There are many notions to mask it, not the least of which is philosophy. But what kind of man sits at a bar drinking when the world is filled with beautiful women, when they stride the Saturday afternoon streets in the finery they paid for themselves, when the light shines from all their colours of hair more brightly than the most vivid of constellations and their legs stretch up and down in sunlight's sliding glamour? A man who has given up, a man beaten by experience, a weak man. A pitiful pathetic man. But then . . . perhaps it's all in the show, like the girlie show. Perhaps even the most pampered and preened metrosexual is the biggest tosser in a capacious ballbag.

When I see Hopper's woman I see a million women in this country, parading at the bottom of the bed for their fat farting husbands, husbands who'd probably divorce them if they could get their hands on a younger piece of fluff. Now I've been divorced four times, and I think they found younger women three out of four, maybe four times. The last bastard said I had become *embittered*. Now what the gives that little shit the right? I did that nightly parade and men have always loved it. He was a two minute eye drop.

We're all ageing strippers centre stage. The wisest of us can render naked the most complex of attire. Society is filled with physical nakedness, or near to nakedness. It's a metaphor for the fucking obvious. If a man just walks in the door and stands there naked parading the last risen rooster am I supposed to immediately accommodate him? Why must we all endure this cultural dumbshow, this all too obvious and ultimately narcissistic parade? *Girlie Show* is a picture to some up our times now, when everyone believes they themselves have the X factor, and because it's unquantifiable it's another in a long line of marketing tools for the unquantifiable, the appropriation of a poetic conceit for the fist fucking purposes of a committee.

God it takes me a long time these days. My arse is freezing. Let me flush. Right, back downstairs. I need a drink now, it's gone eleven, good. Come with me to the cocktail cabinet. Whisky, vodka, gin, Bloody Mary, Gin? Okay, gin. Ice and a slice?

Turn around; it's on the wall behind you. Isn't that magnificent? Some people say you can't call Hopper magnificent, but the capture of the ordinary is magnificent, makes manifest the mysteries of existence more than the gold cloth histories of kings and princes. And its significance to me? Well, let me just have a sip of this, get the juices flowing. Let me look, let me look. Keep still now, picture me sitting here looking at the picture, thinking. Picture me, not the picture, now listen and picture the picture in your own mind. Right. Bang! I'm joking; it's much slower than that.

Obvious though, in its way. *Four Lane Road*. *Four Lane Road* is me and my last husband. He is sitting outside smoking a cigar and watching the sunset. The woman has her head sticking through the window, trying to communicate with this monosyllabic, lazy man. She has probably been working hard. He is just sitting there. Now that was him all over. Oh, hang on. I'll get the door.

'What?'

'Can I interest you in the words of Jehova?'

'Oh get to fuck.'

Doe eyed bastards. They only want your money, whatever they say. Piety comes calling and wanks off over your silver. The gentle words of the lost, the crutch of belief, the mug's consolatory belief of an afterlife tinted with roses. Such a panoply of horseshit trombones.

Four Lane Road, so yes, what was I saying? Horace, that son of a bitch. Couldn't ever get a word out of him. He was a builder, and he'd come home from work and he just wouldn't speak, and no matter how long and loud I spoke, there would never be a reply. And that's him, sitting outside in the quiet sunset, smoking a cigar and doing nothing, saying nothing. How can a man just sit there like that, just smoking and doing nothing? Horace would sit in our back garden, on a deckchair, reading the evening newspaper but mainly just smoking. And then he'd open a bottle of wine and take it out into the garden and sit there drinking by himself while I'm stuck inside, clacking my knitting needles and having to talk to myself. That's no way to conduct a marriage. Couples need to communicate. Once he said he wished that I would take a vow of silence. I never let him forget that one.

The thing is with men, right, is that they listen and listen until they get you in bed, and then you make love, and then they go from a horse's tackle (!) to a horse's head. All Horace wanted to do after sex was hug me. Wouldn't speak a word, said there was 'nothing to say', said that the way I spoke 'didn't require a response'. He was a strange man. The only time he ever seemed to speak was to moan about his back. Well that was his own fault. A fifty year old man carrying bricks. You'd have to be pretty stupid to still be carrying bricks at fifty. And Hopper captures that stupidity in *Four Lane Road*. The woman is trying to communicate with an ignorant man who'd rather sit outside smoking a cigar in the sunset that talk to his wife. She is shouting at him, just trying to get a response. He looks scared to me, and Horace was scared too. Why else would a man apply for the job of hermit on a Greek island? Because that's exactly what he did. Sent me a letter a month after he disappeared. He didn't even take any of his stuff. Just left it here to remind me of him. I can picture him now, looking out at the sunset across the sea. On his own in total silence save for the sounds of nature.

In the picture the man is grabbing at the arm of the chair with his left hand. This is fear. It's hard to respect a man who is scared of a woman. In his letter Horace said that I was 'too hard'. Said I wasn't 'feminine' enough. Said he liked a woman to be a woman. Now what the fuck is that all about? He wants me to stay at home all day and do the cooking and ironing and then make myself look good for him when he gets home? I don't think many men would want that. And what would be in that for me? I've never been the property of a man. I never take their name in marriage. That's patriarchal bullshit, not love. I can drink as much as any man. I am strong, I am attractive, and of course I'm feminine. And he's not interested. It's almost like he doesn't even see her physical qualities anymore, has turned his back on them. Well that's his loss. I don't miss him. How can you miss something that doesn't speak? An empty shell. A hollow man. A *Four Lane Road* without any traffic. Just still, smoking, waiting around to die. Well I hope he's happy when he dies alone on that Greek island. 'You can't escape yourself' is what he wrote. Well I know that, I'm not the one who went crying off to a Greek island to avoid the realities of life. It's just like a holiday, you have to come back. Except he never did. Well I'm better off without that shuffle of dust. I never loved him anyway. He thought I did and he said that was the only thing that made it difficult for him to go away. So at least I made him suffer a little bit over that.

Okay so now we're in the kitchen. *Railroad Sunset*. What colours. Let me describe them to you. It starts in blue, moves into impressions of yellow, filters further down into black wires of cloud before the pink red of the sunset strip and one rolling ribbon of green. Then in the foreground there is the light shining on the lines, and the signal box next to the signal post. Now in my life I look at that picture and infer so many things, but the central inference is that I am the signal box sick of giving signals, and I sit there empty looking out at the dazzling horizon sunset where all the life of the world is.

We'd known each other before. But by the time we got back together he was married to someone else, and they had a child and a home and a wholly settled scenario he would never leave. I was his excitement, the receptacle for his white moaning, the mug who listened to all his complaints about the wife he would never leave. And he began to blame me for having seduced him when it was me weighed down by his gifts of flowers and perfume and ridiculously elaborate lingerie.

But it was such an illusion, a carefree unthinking joust in hotels, on hillsides, in his car. And after a while his just leaving started to shiver me. To think of him home, kissing his family, falling asleep in his wife's bed while I was alone washing him out of me in the shower, well that began to leave me with an empty space where my soul used to be. And I know it wasn't easy for him, but I know it was harder for me.

One thing that seemed only part real were the telephone conversations. They had started in the same way and progressed. It was the way we could thrill each other with our voices. It would start with a charade of commonplaces, but then the timbre of our voices, our deliberate taking of them to a certain pitch, would mean that we listened to ourselves slowly undressing. He told me he was sat right under the front window of his house (a place we'd made love) and that anyone passing by might be able to see him but that he didn't care. I could hear the zip on his trousers, the slow stroking that would increase in speed. For my part I would whisper expletives, say the dirtiest things I could imagine him doing to me, put the handset between my breasts, lift my nipples from the cups and circle them with the tips of my nails. He would tell me how hard he was and I could hear him stretching out and stroking, and I would then reach into my knickers and start to touch where it was already wet, and slowly, all the time listening to his dirty deep voice that I knew was only an act, I would start to slide my fingers along it, tap it, brush it, gently flick it so that I was writhing around, and then I'd put the phone down to piss him off. I didn't want to hear him. I liked the illusion, didn't want to hear the sad reality. And then it occurred to me that he was probably using me as foreplay before going to bed with his wife, and so we didn't do that anymore.

And then of course it came time for him to make a decision, and despite all the promises I think I always kind of knew what that decision was going to be. It's like you know the end is bad almost before the beginning but your body takes over your head because the whole size of that tingling takes over your brain, and you take the trip and you take the rip, and leave with nothing but a rapidly diminishing memory of physical sensations because of the inevitable break in what some small part of you, the part of you rusty from unthinking, still hoped would be a continuum.

He was *such* a handsome man. And he had this way of looking at me that made my breasts tingle. And I

love a man in a suit, with big polished shoes and a nice
car to pick you up in. And he had this big fat gold
watch that burst up through his cuffs, and a big old
wedding ring. And his clothes always seemed so new,
as though he'd bought them just to wear for me, crisp
cotton boxers and clean smelling socks, pristine white
shirts and the lovely, freshly moisturized skin on his
face just prickling with a grey shadow that matched
the hue of his suit in the mornings. And I have to say
that I love the way he left on those mornings, with
that stubble, and his hair all ruffled, and his tie hanging
loose around the collar, and it was funny but with him
I kind of liked the fact that he knew there was nothing
to say, and he didn't have to fill the silences with commonplaces to assuage some deep seated or even temporary insecurity. And I'd watch from the window of my
flat as he got in the car and sped off without so much
as a backward glance. It was a gaudy yellow sports car.
I don't remember the make, and it surprises me that I
could like a man who drove a yellow car, but it's vivid
to me now, the way it whizzed down the city centre
street, kept stopping at lights before whizzing off again,
a bright speed of yellow under mizzling grey. And yes,
Railroad Sunset brings all of that and a thousand more
memories back to me of that time, and though it's
in the kitchen I wouldn't say I look at it every day,
but the days I do, maybe when the light through the
windows throws a certain shade of gilt onto the frame,
I get a resonant thrill from the colours and a corre-
sponding sadness from the signal box.

What else have I to show you . . . there are a few
more Hopper's but, wait, I know. Now this isn't quite
in the script, but it's a picture that I have here above

my desk. Not a Hopper, but an influence on Hopper: *A Bar at the Folies-Bergère* by Édouard Manet. Now I told you before that I had been a barmaid and this painting, and the barmaid in it, just sums that job up perfectly to me.

Everyone around you is having fun, or trying to have fun, or seeming to have fun, except the sad sacks at the bar who only look at you when they think you can't tell. But you *feel* them. You feel their lonely eyes like a trail of gunpowder across the bar and up the back of your legs and up your back and burning into your bra straps. To me the girl in the painting has the innocent eyes of a barmaid not long in the job. I was that way; a million girls before and since have been that way. She's beyond the novelty that comes at the start and before the hardness that comes with longevity. She is at that middle stage when she is beginning to see something of the human race that her youth in secret gardens didn't know. But her innocence hasn't been exploited yet and so her comprehension is only slightly emerging from his cosset. She is prey for the waiting, perhaps the man in the moustache in the mirror whose eyebrows are a masquerade of good intentions but whose mind his filled with her doe eyes and the exquisite décolletage time will make a half hearted display. I myself would kiss her honeyed breasts in the burnished furnace of life, for soon that expression will be locked away forever and her own furrowed brows and the encroaching crow's feet and cellulite and stretch marks that her future holds will overtake her mirror, and her body will be like the décolletage in that the flowers will be withering, and the fruit in the bowl beside her will be shrivelling and shading and she will have four marriages and the experience of four different myriads of mistakes but those mistakes will all come together to make her ache for even more love, so that approaching middle age such fires to burn out a tank torment her waking nights and days, wet her, so that she will come full circle and melt for a man in a top hat with a moustache and innocent eyebrows.

VIGILANTE MAN

Everyone else has had their say. Now it's my turn. I'm a family man. My duty is to protect my family. I make no excuses for what I did, but I'd like to try and help you understand why I did it. I don't disturb anyone else. I work hard to pay for my house and my car. At first I didn't notice when they started damaging the car. My wife pointed to a scratch on the passenger door and I thought that maybe I'd done it while driving. Then the wing mirrors were smashed off and the tyres were slashed. I looked out of the window one night and saw them jumping up and down on the roof. When I went out they ran off and I could hear them laughing. After I reported it to the police all they said was that I should have reported the earlier incidents. They kept saying that over and over. I ended up feeling like it was my fault. I couldn't tell who the kids were because of the hoods. The police said I should have reported the earlier incidents, but I still think getting the police involved was the worst thing I did. After that is when it went worse. Like I've said before, I've no idea why they were picking on me and my family. We've never done anything to anyone. It's scary when you're watching the telly and someone throws a golf ball at your front window, and it's even scarier when they throw one at your bedroom window in the middle of the night. You pay someone to repair the damage in the morning. Then it happens again. They started shouting at my daughters, saying all kinds of things I don't want to repeat here. It's hard to explain. All these things just build up in your head. You spend all day and all night angry, you can't sleep. Every time the police came round it was as though I was wasting their time. I found out a name of one of the lads and I told the policewoman and I asked her if the lad had a criminal record, and she said she couldn't tell me that. This woman said that for all she knew I might have a criminal record too. It's hard to believe. So what it is is that we all get treated the same way, even though as we've heard he has a criminal record as long as his arm. I've never even gone overdrawn at the library. How is this right? When I was a teenager I bet I was bored too, but I didn't smash people's cars up or throw golf balls at their windows or shout obscenities at young girls. I didn't walk around with a hood covering my face. Why do they want to hide their faces unless they're doing something wrong? This isn't me being paranoid. I'm a rational man. I just wanted to protect my family. It's ironic that I'm on camera. The camera's I paid out for show these little — sorry, show these lads — with their hoods up, running around on my drive and on the street nearly every night. Everybody knows it's them but we can't do anything about it. But now I didn't have a hood up you can see it was me. I'm not violent, but it builds up, it becomes all you can think about, and the police can't do anything, there's so many things they can't do it's a waste of time. We all have to wait until someone actually gets shot or knifed or something. And then there's all this rehabilitation, all these theories, all these daft liberal ideas to rehabilitate them. They need to be punished. These weren't children who didn't know what they were doing. Teenagers are old enough to know the difference between right and wrong aren't they? Don't their parents teach them anything these days? We're too nice to them. It was the thing with Barney that flipped me. I just couldn't comprehend how someone could knife a dog. There's a scar all along his side and the fur hasn't grown back yet. He doesn't even bark anymore. It stills gets to me, and you know, I'm sorry to say it, but I'd do it all again. Except this time I wouldn't just smash their legs. I don't feel guilty when I see their parents here, I'm sorry, I just don't. Do your worst. I don't expect you to be able to understand. You'll probably take them lot on some holiday somewhere. And you'll probably lock me up and leave my family without a husband and a father. I know you'll say I should have thought of that, but I wonder what it's like where you live. I doubt you have any idea of what I'm really talking about, sat there all calm. But should we all just have to lock ourselves up in our houses and be scared all the time? These kids know that they can get away with it. I just think we're too kind to them and they need to be punished for what they do wrong. I lost my temper, I admit that, but I only lost it after a long long time, a time when nobody could help me to sort things out. Even if you forget all the months leading up to it, the smashed windows, the slashed tyres, the verbal abuse, just remember that they knifed my dog. They knifed my dog. I'd break their legs again. That's all I have to say.

ARRAN SONG

for John G Hall

The top hills of Arran were held in mist. The blue sky filled with cirrus clouds held back over the black waves. Salt water of the largest waves splashed across the front of the ferry. Holy Isle was black under a black cloud as the ferry slowed over swells into the terminal.

There was a queue outside the bus so he walked along the sea front at Brodick before heading inland towards Glen Rosa. He put up his tent by the rising river. Lying on top of his sleeping bag he listened to crows, seagulls, blackbirds, swifts, swallows, ringed plovers, grouse, curlews and later the ghost of a cuckoo call.

In the toilet there was a birds' nest. When he went into the toilet a swallow swooped in and checked on her chicks in the eaves. Directly under the nest — on the floor between the urinals — there was a small black and white mound.

Near the tent he stopped by flowers. While waiting for a red and brown and black patterned butterfly to open its wings he watched as it retracted its tongue from nectar; the tongue curling up like a tiny fire hose.

On the way out, by the rubbish bins, he saw a red squirrel skipping through litter.

≈

He went up the clear path to Goat Fell, passing cloud berries, bog myrtle, bilberry, yellow pimpernel, speed-well, asphodel and star of bethlehem. In the sky ahead he saw a buzzard. The broad spanned wings of its rolling flight held some of the same sylvan colour as the butterfly's wings. Back on the path he noticed a shiny green beetle, lifted it, felt it, placed it gently back in the heather. On the summit his eyes were dreams of blue corolla.

He descended to Corrie from North Goat Fell. Ravens hovered above him and landed on the rock where he'd lunched. They were like friends you'd make anyway. In their black flight something of the heavens was contained. The ridge path ran untouched in the dustless air.

As a boy he'd dropped litter on the streets of Kil-winning, but on walks in the country he'd always taken rubbish home, rubbish that included banana skins, bread crust, apple cores. Under the reproachful flight of ravens he thought of leaving something behind.

He heard a deer and looked up for the spot of brown in rocks, waited for the deer to move but it didn't before he did. He saw a golden eagle fly in from the sea, over his head then over the ridge behind him. He looked for the shadow of a hump backed whale in the blue silver beyond the glen. There was an osprey. At Corrie he had a pint in the pub and watched for otters from the beer garden on the shoreline, thought he saw them in the movement of wave. He walked down the road a while and then back on to the teeming shore, smelled the salt air, skimmed smoothed stones across the water, squinted at gannets crashing down for fish. He heard the tire tracks of luminous cyclists above the brushing waves. He thought he saw somersaulting otters but it was the sea bumping and jumping over rocks. He walked to a bench, sat and waited. He looked at an anchored oil tanker and the low cloud above it. Car tyres curled over the gravel behind him. He got up and walked away.

A helicopter buzzed over the Sound of Bute, over wind farms, over Ardrossan harbour, over a lighthouse, over quickening glitter, under porcelain blurs of cloud, then again over the bluenesses of Bute. Three girls laughing on bicycles circled the coast road. In the water, a girl in a green bikini walked along dragging a boat behind her. When the girl in the boat was gone he stripped to his shorts and waded into the water. He did breast stroke, back stroke, crawl. He felt the seaweed and the warm currents from the Gulf Stream, tasted the salt. He reached through the water for sand and did handstands. He swam blinking through the sunlight on the sea. He wouldn't leave the paradise of the gentling water and swam in circles until the sun fell behind the houses that lined the road that ran around the island's shore. When eventually he came trembling out under the emerging starlight he saw that the incoming tide had taken his trainers. The salt water droplets on his body reflected pin points of the moon. A woman with kinky curls collected swan feathers by the shore.

At Kingscross he walked around clementine coloured jellyfish and looked over at Holy Isle. The squat white lighthouse sat backed by two white houses and the green rise up to the higher rocks and cliffs. An oys-

75

tercatcher flew from right to left and back again, the perfect symmetry of its elegantly rushing wings seeming to brush the scanned over surface. Two oystercatchers played around together, running and jumping, red bills vivid and calling loudly to distract him from the nest only yards away.

Looking to his left across the bulk of Holy Isle and back around he could see the range of peaks and the ridge of high hills rising over Lamlash, the highest, Goatfell, to the right of the rocky vista, clouds around it like a bush fire or dust balls.

He jumped into the surf and swam halfway across, resting a few minutes on a red buoy. On Holy Isle he sat shivering on the sand and rose to run up and down in the heat of the sun. His whole body was pink, glowing. The sting of a jellyfish told him the same thing. He looked at Arran, swam back faster.

Walking over the pebbles and shoreline rocks, he climbed back up to a grassy ledge, felt the soft grass under his feet, lay back, stuck to it, dried under the sun and the flight of white butterflies. As his breathing slowed and the rising and falling of his chest became almost imperceptible, he looked at the purple skies and sparkling stars that filled the vision of his closed eyes.

He looked at the sunset shining on the hull of an anchored tanker in the sound, and knew that memories could be a concept of heaven too. Memories embedded in the graces of Arran; in skies sad as cello songs, in the coruscating granite of hills, in the manifest glories of sea light through the windows of a yellow church.

CITY SUNLIGHT

He's been up all night drinking coffee and filling rolls of teletype paper. As the traffic gets louder and the yellow hue rises up off the puddles and glints off the old stone walls he smokes a cigarette and feels his back and wipes the sweat from his brow and flexes his knee and looks up at the yellowing ceiling but he can't relax yet, he has to go out into it all, keep the feeling and so he does and he goes out and the city sunlight is filtering between the tall buildings and the wind is blocked but comes down the canyons of avenues and he wonders where to go what to do and just walks through the town and the city and he looks at all the faces, knowing death had undone so many but with his kind heart not judging them and so he walks and sits on 42nd for a while with a shoe shine man then walks to the park and sees all the finery of the city walking their dogs and he thinks it's time for a drink so he goes to get a brown bag with a bottle in it and sits with a wino in a shadow of the Queensborough bridge, watches the sunlight shining on the Hudson, sees tugboats going by, waves at them, waves the bottle at them and the wino tells him he looks like a movie star and they both drink and the drink gives an aura to the sunlight, a poetry to the light on the water, a poetry to the shadow of the bridge on the water, a poetry to jogging; gives poetry to things that had poetry

before and poetry to things that didn't and anyway it
just makes him feel poetic, he drinks for joy and the
whole world is a joy in this, the young life, the greatest
moment before his big success when he's still stuffed
with the thrill of it, hasn't yet become what he won't
be able to escape and he gives the smiling wino the
bottle, looks at his red face, red from sun and booze,
and sees the smile and walks away taking the smile, the
romance, the drunkenness and he looks back out at the
Hudson and thinks of Frisco Bay and the Pacific Ocean
at Big Sur and he thinks of the crossing to Japan and he
thinks of Buddha and he thinks of women with roses
for breasts, he thinks of all the gone poetry of cities, he
walks knowing something of what he's done in the old
hotel, knows it's new, knows it will change the world
or be noticed at least, not like the first one he carried
around in a satchel for so long and for what? And he
doesn't yet know of the editorial genius to help him,
but maybe has some intimations in it from the flowing
words of America he's got down night after night for
the last three weeks in one mad rush of glory when
all the saints and sinners and apostles and the paintings of saints in chapels and chapel crosses all came to
him in benediction and pots and pots of coffee and he
got words down to last like red words on stained glass
windows, stained glass windows that lasted through
two world wars of critics and shone down on all the
people that read them; all those ordinary people who
perhaps knew nothing of Eugene Gant, knew nothing
of anything in the fifties except that the war was over
and the world was black and white written in black
and white prose until the Technicolor iron giant came
out from the caves of Lowell to capture the light and

love of a soul filled landscape of all colours and lights on a road trip looking for life itself, and he knows something of that as the wine fills his body with that red love of the world, that red yet to be corrupted soul, and the drinking is in the first flush, the first satisfaction, the first thirst of a labourer after eight hours work but for him just eight hours typing, and what typing! typing from the heart, doubling and tripling from the soul, not too censored by parochial concerns, censored if at all by the knowledge that the words were going to be in one of the books of forever and people would come, year after year, to walk past the old hotel where he sat in dust and sweated on dust and in the must of the window frames just went for it, inspired in the mad dog rush of divinity, the flow of his reason for being, the words that killed him and kept him alive forever. And so he walks around the city, walks around in the city sunlight all the time filling with more words of flailing glory and he walks and smokes and drinks and it all goes into him to come out of him again later and back to base looking up at the black metal balconies of the hotel, he goes back in smiling, gets the elevator up, gets back in his room leaves the door swinging in the breeze throws back the drapes and widens open the windows and strips naked and hangs his clothes on the back of the chair and looks at the rolls of type flickering, blowing, fired in the breeze and lies on the grimy sheets and stretches out diagonally across the bed and to the sounds of the city all filling the room with the racket of traffic and falls asleep under the warm oblong of a patch of city sunlight sleeping the sleep of a coruscated pure hearted angel saint.

ANGELS FLIGHT

I remember a time of rooming houses and crack eyed landladies, shiftless tenants; a time of high windows and dreams from Bunker Hill; a time when the bold and the beautiful were nowhere to be seen, except maybe the bold, but that was a boldness you'd recognize then, not a boldness anyone would recognize now. The beautiful, well, they all think they recognize that, but it's a stretch.

I worked the funicular, parked my car at the top of Hill Street, took tourists up and down there on their Chandler and Fante and Bukowski pilgrimages; took a million other people up there until the accident. One day they say it's going to open again, but I'll believe that when I see it.

I live in the Sunshine Apartments, and can see from my window the incline where Olivet and Sinai used to criss-cross. I can still see Olive Street too. But Sunshine Apartments is kind of a joke, because even before the urban redevelopment plan the sun went down early on Bunker Hill. There's a load of old films that show the funicular too. I've seen *The Turning Point, Night Has A Thousand Eyes, Impatient Maiden* and *Kiss Me Deadly*. *Impatient Maiden* starts with an opening scene on the porch of the Sunset Apartments, in *Turning Point* William Holden meets someone here and they end up hiding from hoodlums in a doorway.

I worked one time in the Million Dollar Building but got laid off from that too, and then I had my time in the post office. Days go by and I sit in my room on a diet of boiled eggs and oranges and milk, the thin yellow light comes in through thin blowing curtains and I read mostly Chandler, lose track of the plots but love the cynicism and similes. A hot wind comes in most days, in winter there's sometimes snow but never so much as I remember.

I look at the funicular and there's nothing but the drive round or your own leg power to get you up there where the money is on California Plaza. I remember the old days of boiled cabbage and fish heads and carrots, before most of all the poor were buried in the foundations of the high rise, when even the poor men wore suits and polished their shoes, even if the shoes had cardboard in them; and I remember that it was a nasty place to live, filled with people who'd smile at you at while fondling a blade in their pocket. Now it seems like there's just tourism, and most of all that is hung on the velvet ropes uptown. Even Angels Flight itself is a rebuild, and the guys who re-built it disappeared too when the old man went flying down there.

The irony of this city's name is so profound it takes your breath. But I romanticize it because that is what helps me see the light through the windows the way I do, helps me with my walker to the john in the night though most of me wants to keep sleeping. I like to think of Angels Flight as the part of downtown where, despite the odd accident, a million and more ordinary people were taken higher into the city. And the angels flight itself is the angels flight of directors and movie stars and writers too — remembered or forgotten — who got this place down in a film or a book, captured it for the past and at the same time secured their own flight. Like the funicular itself it wasn't where it took you but how it took you there; and it wasn't about speed and accessibility and the practicalities that reduce transport and all travel to a template of tickets and timetables. It took you there in style, with remnants of romance in the air like flowers giving of their last, when engineering and architecture had designs on permanence and class and it wasn't all about light and glass but holding the dark in angles and corners; the dark of downtown in a time of hats and long dresses and sultry smoking women; women who kept the goods covered but smiled at you in a way that told you that you were both a millisecond and a million miles away; told you how it was all waiting for you if you could only set it up right; and you sat together and looked from the cable cars, felt the musty air cooling slightly with your gradual ascent up Angels Flight, smelt the perfume of a woman framed forever in dusty reels.

NIGHTHAWKS

He was born in a slum by the St George River. Like most of the boys and girls on the crowded and ramshackle street he spent his youth kicking punctured footballs. He liked his time alone with the ball, kicking it against a wall to get it back and control it, or flicking it up and setting a new record for volleys.

When Brazil were knocked out of the 1982 World Cup by Italy in the quarter finals, after they'd been favourites for the tournament, and Humberto saw his favourite player, Falcao, walking off the pitch defeated, something in the boy was lost too. For though Brazil would go on to have many more great players and win world cups again, there was something about that special team not winning the tournament that stayed with Humberto, made him lose his love for sport, took away the edge he'd need for footballing success.

He began to gaze from the littered hillsides towards the silvered ships on the polluted waters of the harbour, where oily waves made washed out rainbows either side of prows that ploughed forth in the export of coffee and bananas.

Humberto studied hard, found he was good at remembering things and excelled in exams. He escaped Santos and moved away to live in the futuristic capital of Brasilia.

Leaving his office he would visit the Catedral Metropolitana de Brasilia, where he'd stand under the sculpture of angels descending. But the beauty of Brasilia seemed forced, all too deliberate, too much an abuse of the best instincts of art, and he escaped it by taking his holidays in the Serra Da Canastra national park.

He camped in the riparian forests along the Sao Francisco River, studied his guidebook and looked through his binoculars for the many species of birds: white striped warbler, black masked finch, white rumped tanager, ochre breasted pipit, helmeted manakin, cock tailed tyrant, Brasilia tapaculo, Brazilian merganser, stripe breasted starthroat. He'd climb high into the hills and look at the ghostly vapour that filled the valleys like a dreamscape.

The tree coloured plumage and darkness hid the nighthawks, but every night he knew they were there, could hear the squeaking and squelching of their trilling as it broke gently past other intimations. He lay in his tent listening and images came forth: the punctured ball rolling around in the dust of the wasted kicking years, the sunlight suffused on the thickened waters of the bay, the ships off and away through the waves, his mother in her broken shoes as he led her from the slum to the tiny house he bought her and then left her behind to die in, the local girls like a book of stories that excitement made him rush through in order to get to the end and go back too late; stories of girls with crow black hair and olive skin, and the special one he left like he left his mother, as he rushed off filled with ambitions that missed the point on the long trip to the simulated beauties of Brasilia.

And there was the memory of the woman in Brasilia who reeled him in time after time on the same dumbly dazzled stretch of his life, the one so driven she couldn't see beyond the confines of her spotless loft apartment and its Oscar Niemeyer views, or her own career, or the image of her increasingly painted face in the many mirrors looking back. And he saw Falcao, sprinting in wild celebration as Brazil went 2–1 up against Italy: the frenzied face, the blown back curly blonde hair, the popped up veins all over his adrenaline filled arms.

One night, Humberto lay outside his tent in the riparian forest of the Serra de Canastra national park, looking up at the beauteous changing colours of the evening sky. With the moon seeing off the sun, and the stars fixed between the branches of the overhanging trees, he put his hands behind his head and kept watching. At first they were just a series of quick shifting shadows, but as his eyes adjusted he began to pick them out more clearly, so that the thrill of their flight lifted him from the ground. He floated among the trees, watching nighthawks catching moths in the moonlight.

EAGLE ON A CACTUS

A nd so I got laid off. Had to sign on. Spent my days going to Stockton and back on the Transporter Bridge. You should see it, man, the sun shining on the Tees, the sun shining through the blue metal bars, the light in the water, the light on the metal, the carrying cables in the rain. My own thing in my own time and over the Infinity Bridge too.

I drank one night a week. Shithole in the shadow of the A19. Mackham's in there. Pool. Smoking hookers. Skinny Asians counting money over kebabs in their cars. I came home cained to the Mrs and the bairns. A washing line of rabbits in the moonlight.

Had a bit on the side in Nunthorpe. Husband played the bongos for P&O. She looked like Jamie Lee Curtis. Got home to her place from The Dickens. Twisted sister was with us. Ancient. Sat staring, unblinking, enough perfume for a thousand Friday nights in O'Neil's. So Jamie Lee made something in a wok and we all had it and by the time I got Jamie Lee to bed I fell asleep with my head between her legs. In the morning she dumped a full English in my lap. I got up and had a coffee and hung my coat and kissed her breasts until Christmas.

Two weeks into the New Year and I was drunk in the afternoon and flying. It's when you haven't got a job or money that you need a drink the most. I walked to Jamie Lee's house. Her kids were at school and she stood at the sink. I cupped her breasts as she washed the pots. She had a black sports car. Took me speeding home in it via a shaking stop on the windy, cloud-busting expanses of the North York Moors. Husband hit me outside the chippy.

Sat in a blues club in sunglasses, fondling my silver harmonica. Joined in on the open mike to a Jimmy Reed tune about his boss. Ran out of money but got applause and four pints out of a weighty old belter who cried tangles of wet mascara.

I made the dole last a week. Second week was rabbits and stolen milk and family allowance and TV. When Jez told me about the student houses I joined him.

Most of them lived around Linthorpe and Ayre-some Park where the Boro used to be, and Jez told me how they had parties and just left their doors open and all you had to do was try the door in the morning, go in and get the TV's and DVD players and laptops and that. And we did until we got done for it. One time we came out with a violin and a tuba and a xylophone and got wrestled to the floor by a couple of fluorescent puberty police with mountain bikes and the xylophone tinkled on the paving stones. So now I've got a record. Textile industry was replaced by computer technology and I got laid off from both and now all of that is gone anyway. And even if I wanted a job in a call centre I couldn't get one as I'm bobbins on the blower.

In the nick after the job I read loads of books and they had this one in the library about Mexico: Conquista-dors sailing the high seas in the 15th century searching for gold and spices. Montezuma, Cortes, Machu Picchu and Lake Titicaca. And these guys the Aztecs. They looked for a golden eagle perched on a cactus, devouring a snake. There was something on the telly too. I could while away the hours with that, and the westerns set in Mexico. Amigos and desperadoes and gringos and bastardos. I would have fit right in there. Give me a silver palomino and a poncho and a bottle of whisky and let me ride to a whorehouse where those black haired and brown eyed and golden col-oured whispering wenches could feed on enchiladas and tequila with my fistful of dollars.

I got this job as a window cleaner. Some kind of joke by the probation. Let me look in at the latest high def TV's, let me climb a ladder and look at jewellery, let me close those open windows so I can clean them. It's an early start but they said you just give them all a quick wipe and your quid's in. But I do a proper job. I don't get it but they're scared when we knock on the doors. Only one or two old bruisers complain. And it's all legal. But man, some mornings I don't want to do it. I'm a slave to the system now; I'm free but my freedom's gone. Work all week and go to the pub on Friday's, maybe still get a bit of knock off but that's about it.

After a bit I'd saved up enough to buy a car Golf from a garage in Acklam. I used to drive around at night, relaxed between the white lines and cats' eyes. Nowhere to go but somewhere else that didn't look the same. One time I went over to Durham, all the windows down and listening to Sonny Boy William-son. Another time I drove to Redcar and watched the surfers in the summertime running over the beach to the sea.

I loved that Golf and I washed a lot of windows and stayed in on Friday's to get it, so in the middle of one night when it seemed like a little hoodie was trying to get the door open I grabbed him and shoved him to the floor. I ripped the hood off his head and was about to give him a good kicking when I saw his frightened face. Little freckle faced sod barely out of school. Told him that I worked for that car and he got a knife out but dropped it and ran off and I let him go.

The council got us a flat and I've signed up for a night class at college. At night I look out of my window at the car and beyond. The towers of the chemical plant sparkle. Smoke drifts in patterns through the lights, and flowers of flame take me away from soapy buckets and shiny ladders and shammy leather. And in the depths of sleep I have another dream: I'm in Oaxaca as the church bells ring, flying with Cortes and the conquistadors, smelling the flowers over gravestones, floating among skulls and photos and candles and oranges, tasting mescal in the silver moon as the mariachi bands play.

TEENAGE SONGS

When he was a child he smiled his uncondi-
tional smile, rarely cried, made up words by
the dozen, kissed girls and boys alike, laughed until it
seemed to curl his hair. The neighbours loved him,
the teachers loved him, we, of course, loved him. We
gave him everything he wanted, believing it better
to spoil than disappoint. He was gifted at all sports,
did well enough in classes, had his first girlfriend at
eight years old. I remember the Christmas he shot up,
and the long fingers he pushed into goalkeeper gloves
before velcroing them closed around his thickening
wrists. I remember when he first said no, the first time
he came up with his own ideas. I remember the first
time he looked at me with disappointment in his eyes.
I remember the punches we exchanged at the top of
the stairs. I remember how we never once hugged
each other, never once had an adult conversation.

*I kept the truth of my life in silent places where the white walls
were lost and eagle's wings caught the sun in a series of spec-
taculars. Nights in the grass followed such days in the sun and
passages of wonder came and went in the wonderful whispers
of the sheaves. For some the truth comes in days and nights
just numbers while for some of us it had to be held like razors
inside our fists. For it was only in such times we touched the
wires, climbed the stars, ran in front of trains like bored boys*

in dead towns knowing. We caught those who came with us
for as long as we dared, then let them pass in rushing. For us
in the red skies locked for combat with angels and flying devils
our blood flowed golden as sunlit cider, our eyes were red with
excess, the calm of our lives came when we guessed the final
way to beat the game.

This is what he left us. No videos, DVDs, just some
curled photographs and this note. All around this town
they were doing it.

We meet together sometimes, to talk over drinks
about what we have in common, but the night ends
in men and women crying, men and women fighting,
men and women in bed together sleeping off their
losses alone.

I take this note to my heart for his brother and sister,
and when I'm working again I'll try to take something
from it and continue to live.

I can't say what I want to of him in words, but he's
in our heads and in our hearts and in our souls, and
that, and his brother and sister, and mother, well, they
are what stop me from screaming.

I was in the boozer with one of the other dads. He
pulled out a folded piece of paper:

It's grey skies and grey walls and grey faces and suffering in
silence because nobody will talk and it's the smell of piss in
all corners of the walls and its money and ambition. It's black
dogs. It's the bricked heads of toddlers by the railway tracks.
It's epileptic fits in parka's. It's cutting. It's the rain. It's the
darkness under a railway bridge when the streetlight has gone.
It's smashed bus shelters and burned out cars. It's needles on

the stairs. It's the smiling bastards with beer cans. It's shaved heads. Tattoo's on faces. It's the wind through the windows. It's the broken bikes on the balcony. It's the man in the shop. It's the shop. It's the shit blowing about on the streets. It's the shit people throw from their windows. It's the women getting into dark cars. It's the motorway at night. It's the sirens. It's the glasses smashing. It's the wolf whistling. It's the fear, the walking, waking fear. It's the beer. It's the cheaper than water beer, and the vodka on the grass, the vodka on the concrete and swings, and the glass in the concrete and the graffiti on the swings. It's the faces of people on the street not looking. It's nothing. Nothing. It's a waste of fucking time. A waste of FUCKING TIME.

To me I think these kids just can't cope with the emotion of life. Something like that. Like the way we look back on being teenagers now. Remember how you felt then? You can't really, none of us can. But I remember that it just didn't seem so bad after a while. I always just felt better after a few pints. Sometimes certain things hit you, like birthdays, but not just that.

I wish I could shake him by the shoulders and tell him that life is *fucking joyful.* But it's too late and I'm not sure now. But I know that we loved him and he knew we loved him. We loved him. And the others all loved their boys and girls too. And still do. I can see that. You must believe that. Nothing left but flowers. And they get stolen, sometimes. I go back and check.

One of the mothers showed me this:

Night. I can hear wind in the tree. The footfalls of cats on the grass. Your glass, dad's can. An aeroplane going to who knows where. Probably coming back. Now I can hear the wind in the tree again. But they cut the tree down. There's a car. No more trains, no more line. Just footballs and condoms and blackberries and rats. I can hear the computer. I touch it. The old messages stay in the same lines. It's all there. I save this now. Someone is walking along the street. Their shadow will show on the pavement. The wind rattles the streetlight. The white pole of the streetlight will be wobbling. The cat flap goes. The wind has stopped.

WHY I DON'T HAVE LOVE

Three months ago I met a woman in town, but I don't remember anything about the night I spent with her. A short time afterwards I received this letter:

Dave (Fuck You)

You have to read because it very important to you..Thank you for not calling. When you fuck me you sperm still inside my puzzy and I think I am going to have a baby with you.. At first I wanted you to take me to see a doctor to stop pagnantcy, but you don't answer telephone. I have deicided to keep our baby. I will revenge you..After 9 months you should prepare to be a new father..After 2 months I will go to the hospital for blood check because I am going to have our baby..I will write to you for the blood resule..If I have the blood+ I wil still keep our baby because it your. If you don't believe it's your baby take it to the hospital for checking. The DNA..for sure 100% It's you..I'am not fucking joking with you..I'am not joking..I hope you won't move to new apartment..You have to responsible what you Fucking Did..I will leave the baby with you next door..I hope the baby will look like you.. and don't FUCKING try to call me again. Because I don't want to speak with you..and I don't want to see you too. Remember you told me that you don't fuck around..and why I fuck with you. You was fucking me for many times (all night) without useing condom. You said you can remember

94

me and you said to me many times that you like me and you hoped to see me again So we could go out again..you was very sweet to me remember.

Don't try to call me again. I will contract you when the time come..Do you think is a good REVENGE? I don't forgive you what you did to me..I'am trying to get the govemet apartment near you. If YOU see me around, I don't want to talk to you by anywords..If YOU don't like a baby Please find someone to adopted them..you have responsible Dave (I'am not joking and it not funny) Now I have an employment benefit and get monet for apartmet too..Don't worry I can stay here without anyone..After I have a baby I will try to get a job. I have no one here so I have to lean how to take care myself. My husband left me and you kicked me away of you life. After I have a baby I can get money from the government too U.K. Goverment very very good.

After haveing a baby I will find someone and I hope that he don't like OUR baby for sure. You hate me I know, but please don't hate our baby because they do nothing wrong, and please don't move to another apartment because the baby need father need car and need love I think it not difficult to you to find someone that take care our baby

MY MOTHER SHE LEFT ME IN FRONT OF MY DAD home they didn't stay to gether because my FATHER he's already have a wife So he left me at orphanate house. At there it was a very difficult life. Why I don't have love because I never have love with any people before.

I have a baby with you but with out love it not a problem to me..It's will be your problem. I have no one I have nothing I have nothing to loose and I'am not afraid anything. I am very Brave heart. When You have no one you will know.

Dave you don't know me very well you think I'am stupid

and innocent, I'am harder than you think and I have a strong heart than you are. You will see.

Dave.. TOMORROW MORNING I will go see a doctor, I need their advises because I never have a baby before

I have change my mind If the baby have blue eyes and blond hair I will give it to you. If it look like me I will keep it but I will teach them that their father died by car accident. I don't let them call you _dad_

I THINK YOU DO CARE WHAT THE HELL YOU FUCKING DID it not easy to kick me away Dave and you have to reponsible too..Please be a real man—WAN

P.S. TO FUCKER LIER
When you see me anywhere don't come talk to me. If I see you around I will think you are just someone I used to known

don't expected to see me in the pub again I'am not a drinker. I go to pub just 1-2 time a year

I know we will see each other again by accident. Did you see the white building from yours home . . . that is very near my apartment

If you see me you should think I'am just someone YOU USE TO FUCK FOR FUN O.K. I know you think I'am a possitude but I'll give your baby.

We are staying the same area the city centre is so narrow, probably not because I'am usually stay at home because I have no friends here, no friend than no need to go outside

I am going to devorce my husband soon and I told him already what I fucking did so he will come to Manchester after two weeks to devorce me. I've got married here so I think it not difficult. I called to him and he understood every thing and he hope I will be happy with new baby and new boyfriend. He said if I have any problem he will help me.

I've already ask him to bring me 2000+ pounds and he

said he give me a cheque. He's always nice to me not same as you Dave. You are basterd and SELFCENTRED. You should be wearing a skirt..chicken (you are chicken)

Three months later I received this letter from China:

Dear Dave,
How are you now? I'am not feel very well I've already checked my blood, the doctor told me that I have HIV infection and Hepatitis B.

Now I'am in the hospital, I'am not feel very well, I'am cheated my husband to sleep with you (only you) so why I had an infections, why didn't you tell me the truth that you have infections, Why you lie?

My husband left me, he left me because I told him that I've been sleeping with you, I'am feel guilty.

Now I'am in China, I'am Thai Chiness, I've lived with my father, my daddy is Chiness my mom is Thai, my dad look after me because I always have a very bad headach and feel not very good now.

I have many kind of medisons but medison in China is not very good as medisons in England, the doctor told me that I shouldn't worry but I'am afraid

HIV medison in China is very expensive, I don't know how long can I still alive because my dad he don't have much money, his cloths business is now not very good. Now I'am staying in the hospital for (Hepatitis B) treatment. It's cost my dad a lot, I've been saying here since 2 weeks ago

the doctor told me that I have to stay there at least 1 month, my body is very plan and the doctor put medison in to my hand for 3 liquid medisons a day, It's very hurt but nothing I can do, I also take the medison for HIV

You have to know Dave what you have done to me.

Everybody don't like me to near them because I have a decease, I'am so desolate.

I've already forgiven you Dave, my daddy told me that I should try to forgive, I tell you so you can go see a doctor to the medison treatment, if you don't go see a doctor now it's will be too late for you, you should go see the doctor as soon as possible so the doctor can help you.

I'am tired Dave I have to sleep now, my brain is very plan (headach) and I plain my rib, when I go to the toilet my urine is a very dark yellow, bye— Wan

There were about twenty people waiting, men and women all of a similar age to me. I spoke through the partition and the nurse asked me speak up. I told her I was there for a HIV test.

I waited for a long time and saw one person after another get up and go with the nurse into a room. Some people looked calm and casual, some too casual. All the while the nurse on reception tried not to make eye contact with anyone. In the corner opposite her there was a television showing 'Countdown' and each time I looked at the nurse her eyes moved back to the screen a split second too late.

After two hours my name was called and a nurse took me into a room. She introduced herself and asked me whether I had been to the 'clap clinic' before. She said I looked scared and asked why I had come to see her. I described the circumstances and she took me to another room and sat me in a chair. She asked me if I had a fear of needles and I said no, feeling for that moment a little better. She inserted the needle, rubbed it clean and gave me a little round plaster to cover the hole.

When I went back I told the nurse on reception I had come for the results of my HIV test. After about fifteen minutes a doctor I had never seen before asked me my name and then showed me into a room. He stood in front of the desk looking down at a piece of paper. He motioned me closer and asked me to confirm my name and address. Then he looked down once more at the piece of paper.

OASIS

I 'd swept the walkway clear of fag dimps and gray sands of ash but dust was left in shapes of the brush.

'I thought I'd told you to sweep up?' said Alan, the foreman. 'Do it again and show some heart.'

I pushed the shopping trolley with the bin stuck in it back to where I'd started and pressed down hard and dragged the brush across the floor, wiping out the shapes and putting the dust on the shovel and into the metal bin.

The cool of the summer morning gave way to the heat of the sun that shone in under the shutter doors, and I took my jumper off and hung it on the shopping trolley. My head lolled over the brush as I began to leave patterns of dust again.

The radio with the coat hanger stuck in it played what sounded to me like a self-pitying song by The Smiths. We sat in an assortment of discarded armchairs that when empty looked like a line of school kids waiting to get picked. The idiot DJ cut in with some tabloid gossip. I'd not had time for breakfast so though it was only morning break I opened my Tupperware box and took out the ham and stand at ease and washed it down with coffee from the machine.

'Eh, Baz, are you going to show this lad how to sweep up properly or what?' said Alan.

'It's not complicated is it, really?'

'It looks like a fucking wave machine down there.'

'Laziness, Alan. It's the youth of today, useless.'

'We've fuck all down here so you can give it another try after break,' said Alan.

I swept the walkway clean of patterns as the radio played 'Everybody Hurts' by REM, 'Supersonic' by Oasis, 'Girlfriend in a Coma' by The Smiths, 'Love Will Tear Us Apart' by Joy Division, 'You're In The Army Now 'by Status Quo, and others I didn't recognize or catch the names of in amongst the DJ's vacant banter.

We played darts, either 301 or round the board. When Chris hit yet another winning double he jumped up and down and laughed in all our faces.

'It's not worth getting giddy about is it?' said Baz. 'I mean you've not won out.'

'Pride, Baz. Pride.'

After lunch, Alan shoved the yard brush into my hand and told me to take a bin and shovel out to the alley that ran along one side of the warehouse.

The bricks of the warehouse wall rose a thousand feet up to my right, and on my left in the shadow of the wall there was a smaller wall with shards of glass across the top. I swept up faded fag packets and coke cans, and bags of crisps that rain water fell out of, and looked down the length of the alley. Through the haze I saw what looked like a six foot tall pint of lager. Above me there was a narrow stretch of blue sky and on one side or the other, out of view, the summer sun that gave a bright light I was out of.

I leaned on the warehouse wall and picked idly at a length of moss that grew out from the brick like a green moustache. I held it between my fingers for a moment and tossed it into the bin. A thirst like I'd never known had me by the throat and bits of *Supersonic* re-entered my head.

After kicking the bin over I turned it upside down and jumped on top of it, and then, with my gloved hands carefully picking a space among the shards of glass, I pulled myself up and looked over the wall. Right below the wall, on the other side, a tree branch stuck out like a welcoming arm. I lowered myself back down onto the bin and started sweeping the tipped dust and rubbish back into it again, 'Everybody Hurts' filling my head. My mouth was like the bottom of a budgie's cage and my head was beginning to throb with the need for Alka Seltzer. Supersonic came back. I looked down the alley and the pint seemed to be evaporating before my eyes. I put the yard brush against the wall, tipped the bin up again and jumped over the wall into the tree, before running past a bloke in a little hut in the car park who mouthed something through the glass. As I ran down Fairfield Street a train above me moved away from the platform. I passed The Star and Garter and kept running and saw one of the company wagons on the road. The driver, Billy, gave me a wave and a smile as I looked guiltily back.

I was in the sun now and my thirst was still strangling me so I kept running down Ashton Old Road. A bus went by and on the back of it there was a picture of a palm tree and a pint of lager. I ran after it but it moved further away; the pint getting smaller in the distance. I realized I'd left my Tupperware box behind, but kept running to the sound of the music in my head until I reached The Pack Horse in Openshaw. Either side of the doorway, two topless men with beer bellies and tattoos stared into the sun drinking lager. I went in and got myself a pint and asked the barmaid if it was okay if I took a chair outside. She muttered something back. The two blokes smiled passively and each had another sip of lager. At intervals the 219 passed by on either side of the road and LAGER, in four foot letters, flashed before our eyes.

I wasn't used to the sun, and that and the lager and the smell of petrol was making me drowsy, so I gulped the pint and put my shirt back on and carried on down Ashton Old Road. The traffic got noisier and noisier the nearer I got to home. I went to a cash point in the shadow of a billboard and didn't look up at the picture, and bought four cans from a shop in Fairfield. I kept on walking, the bag of cans banging on my leg.

Near where a new stretch of motorway made a noise that was never there in my childhood, I scrambled up a grassy bank to Audenshaw reservoirs and looked at the sunlight on the water. I walked away from the motorway to the second of the reservoirs where school kids like thrown treasures were arcing into the water off a jetty, passed them and went around to the other side where I sat with a view across the railway line, in a sun trap, with just enough of a breeze to keep me cool. I cracked open a can and put the bag in the shade and drank while looking down at the tracks.

WAVING THEIR SCARVES AT THE SKY

Bacon was crisping under the grill as mum buttered bread. When she saw me, she took the Shreddies from the cupboard and put them on top of the fridge and I got the milk and poured it out through the gap left by the peeled back silver top. I looked out of the kitchen window and saw dad dragging the back gate shut with one hand, newspaper held in the other. On a flowerbed in the shade, Rascal woke and loped onto the sunlit grass before sprawling and closing her eyes again. Dad pushed open the back door, clipped me over the back of the head with the paper, took the bacon butty from mum and then sat on a deck chair in the garden, first eating his breakfast and then reading the news, occasionally pausing to sip from the cup of steaming tea that mum had placed on a brick next to the coal frame.

I sat on the carpet in the living room, watching the TV and waiting for Cup Final Grandstand to begin. Mum sat on the couch smoking a cigarette, the gold packet (complete with warning) on her knee and the familiar smell of Benson & Hedges filling the room on smoke moving slowly to the ceiling.

After I finished my cereals, holding the bowl to my mouth to get the concentrated bits and the rest of the milk, I rushed into the kitchen, put the bowl in the sink and poured myself a glass of orange juice before treading on Rascal's foot, causing her to yelp and all her fur to stand on end. I said 'sorry' over and over and stroked the warm fur down and she moved to her bowl as I went back to the living room and heard the familiar theme tune.

Although there were still hours to the kick off, the build up had already begun in earnest and I watched, rapt, as players in tracksuits were interviewed in their hotel as they sipped orange juice and then later as they all came out of their hotel somewhere outside London, dressed smartly in matching suits and ties. A helicopter followed their route to Wembley and at intervals a camera high in the sky showed the progress of the coach. Then there was the other route to the final — the games that had got both sides there — and I watched again as City, in red and black away kit, defeated Ipswich Town in the semi-final thanks to skipper Paul Power's free kick. After that they showed Spurs' route, finishing on their win over Wolves in their semi final. Then the players of each side were profiled one by one and I remember an interview with City's full back Ray Ranson.

As the coaches got closer to Wembley, the helicopter showed their progress through traffic before panning to the fans already walking towards the Twin Towers down Wembley way, some of them looking up at the helicopter and waving their scarves at the sky. Then it was dinner time and even though City were in the FA Cup Final I still had to go into the dining room to eat at the table, and so missed whatever build up there was during the ten minutes it took me to eat the sausages, baked potato and beans. But at least I didn't have to wash up. Mum did that despite dad's assertion that this was no different to any other day.

As the match kicked off, City in light blue shirts and Tottenham Hotspur in white, dad sat in his usual seat at one end of the couch, white Silk Cut packet (complete with warning) and cup of tea on the table beside, newspaper open on his knee. Mum sat on the two-seater couch on the other side of the room. Minutes into the game she seemed to have already smoked half a dozen cigarettes and the room filled with smoke and the nerves she couldn't hide as well as dad. But even dad threw away the newspaper and jumped towards the ceiling when Tommy Hutchison scored with a diving header.

From that moment and for the rest of the match City seemed to be hanging on, and I remember like it was yesterday (because dad kept saying it over and over), that there were only nine minutes left when Spurs were awarded a free kick just outside the City box. Glen Hoddle curled it around the wall and it seemed that City keeper Joe Corrigan would make it across his line in plenty of time to keep it out, but for some reason Tommy Hutchison had been standing near the six yard box and, in his attempt to block the shot, the ball deflected off his shoulder and into the opposite side of the goal. In the midst of the Spurs celebrations, Joe Corrigan walked over to Hutchison, who was lying on the grass with his head almost buried in the turf, grabbed the back of his shirt and lifted him up. When I looked away from the screen I saw mum lighting another cigarette with the one she hadn't yet finished and dad jumping up and down and calling Hutchison names I'd never heard before.

I think the replay was on a Tuesday night and after tea I went round to my friend Donald's house. When he came out with his ball we ran down the street, passing it back and forth to each other between parked cars. For a while we played outside a factory, swerving and curling the ball into the high gates until I hit one over and had to scale the fence. After the long delay as I struggled back, we carried on running through the streets until we reached a house that had garden gates about the same size as a five-a-side goal and then took turns crossing the ball for each other to score. When cars drove past we'd chip the ball over them for fun. Dribbling down the wing I dodged around an Austin Allegro, did a drag-back past a lamppost, lifted the ball over a kerbstone and chipped the ball across to Donald who thrashed a volley that clipped off the top of the gates and crashed through a bay window to land in an old woman's lap. As we ran off I glanced back to see a grey haired bloke with glasses shaking his fist and behind him the woman in a dressing gown with a red towel wrapped around her head, looking dazed at the Mitre casey.

I don't think we stopped running for a good half an hour and even then we crouched in the dark of an alley near someone's back gate, looking up for the police helicopter we were sure would soon be hovering above. It dawned on us that we'd lost our ball and would have to make do with a flyaway—a ball so light it was liable to go anywhere when you kicked it. We made our way back to Donald's (avoiding the street with the smashed bay window) and climbed the tree in his garden, where we sat and laughed as Donald's sister Cheryl passed naked behind the frosted glass of the bathroom window. Then we remembered the final and I jumped out of the tree, banged my knee on the uneven paving stones and ran home.

The TV threw flickering light into the living room as I sat on the carpet next to the couch to watch. Dad opened a can of lager, mum a packet of cigarettes. As I remember it, after a scrappy, nervous start Tottenham went 1-0 up through their bearded Argentine midfielder Ricky Villa and then City equalized with a volley from Steve McKenzie before going 2-1 up thanks to a Kevin Reeves penalty. Garth Crooks equalized for Spurs, causing dad to kick the unfortunate Rascal (who should have known better than to be in the room) and mum to attempt smoking two cigarettes at once. When Ricky Villa scored again, slotting the ball beneath the onrushing Joe Corrigan, commentator John Motson was in hysterics as Villa ran towards the Spurs fans, arm outstretched in celebration.

Before the end, dad got up, put on his coat and walked out of the back door. Mum said he was going to The Boundary and though I was only eight years old I wondered why that sounded like such a great idea. Later on, in the privacy of my bedroom, I looked for a long time at the souvenir programme from the first game.

I recalled the major incidents of the two matches and couldn't help thinking back to when we'd been nine minutes away from victory. Hours later I heard dad coming home down the quiet street, singing 'Oh, Tommy, Tommy, Tommy, Tommy, Tommy,

Tommy Hutchinson' and I peered out through a tiny gap in the curtains and for the first time noticed the penalty spot on his crown as he picked Rascal up off the garden wall and stood her on his shoulder.

The next day, when dad got home from work, he put a hundred quid on the dinner table. He'd had Spurs in the sweep. When I took the flyaway around to Donald's that night, he said that he was going to become a Spurs fan and I never saw him again, except once in 1987 when a camera picked him out in the Wembley crowd.

PICCADILLY GARDENS

The night before pay day he'd be at the cash point waiting for midnight, and in work later that day people could tell he was drunk because he stank of it and had glassy eyes and there were traces of purple around his lips from finishing the night on rum and black. When there were still gardens in Piccadilly Gardens he'd crash out on a bench under trees and make it into work on time from there.

His name was Eddie Greenhall. He was forty five. His brown hair had turned quickly grey in his early thirties and a circle had emerged on the crown. He didn't love his wife, Mary, and knew she didn't love him, but neither could be alone and getting older. She looked after the kids and sometimes still accommodated his lustful advances. His face was forever red, and his nose a degenerating puce, but she closed her eyes and still needed to feel him, and they made a brilliant disguise of whatever they did like about each other in virulent arguments where Mary always had the last word.

A week after pay day Eddie would have no money left for drinking and so spend the rest of the month in front of the TV, or put on headphones and listen to his Roy Orbison albums. Most nights he'd read to his kids and watch as they succumbed to sleep in the glow of the bedside lamp, before treading lightly down the thinly carpeted stairs to Mary, sat silent and smoking cigarettes in the glow and better company of the television.

The warehouse stocked fixtures and fittings for industrial heating units, and Eddie had been there since leaving school at sixteen. He'd started in telesales but soon realized he didn't like offices and telephones so they put him in the warehouse where he began on picking and packing, then did forklift truck driving until the accident, before coming back as the Goods Inward clerk, where he'd signed for deliveries and checked goods off against invoices for the best part of twenty years.

On the first day working in the warehouse he sat in a dusty armchair next to Tony Alcock, waiting for the foreman Keith Taylor to sort out the delivery notes for the drivers, and watching as drivers and warehouseman loaded steel pipes and oily bags and boxes onto the back of wagons. The steel shutter doors at either end of the warehouse let in the winter and Eddie kicked together the steel toe-caps of his new boots, trying not to look at the hands on the clock that didn't seemed to move above Keith Taylor's head.

Eddie sat next to Tony until morning break, when all the wagons had gone and the shutter doors had been closed and the other warehouse staff went for coffees from the machine in the office. He and Tony had to move onto even scruffier chairs that were less comfortable, and then sat listening to Key 103 on the radio. Some of the other lads read tabloids, some opened Tupperware boxes and ate sandwiches, and others waited until one lad came back from the butty shop, with either egg on toast, or bacon and sausage on toast, or whatever it was they'd asked for. Tony was told he'd be going to the butty shop from then on, and when the bell rang in Goods Inward, Keith told him to get off his arse and answer the door. Later that day someone called Tony 'No Balls' and he was shoved into a shopping trolley, then taped and bound into it with string, before being wheeled out and left behind the trade counter by Eddie, to be laughed at by the blokes waiting in the queue. No Balls found it funny and was happy to help when Eddie and the lads gave the same treatment to those who started in the ware-house after that, the majority of whom could take the joke, save one lad who cried when it came on top of a morning looking for sky nails and glass hammers, and who didn't come back the next day, and who made that next day a bit grim until someone said he was a soft bastard and any guilt left was laughed away.

Sitting at his desk in Goods Inward, with the heater keeping his legs warm and his woolly blue and white striped Oldham Athletic hat covering his ears from the draft through the cracked windows, Eddie fell briefly into thoughts about the big picture of his life, until the bell rang and he got up to keep his finger on the button, watching as the shutter door furled open. He saw the yellow van with the red DHL sign, and the opened back doors and the one female driver that ever came.

'All right, Eddie. Three for you. There's the first two,' she said, pointing to cardboard boxes stacked on top of each other on the floor that Eddie picked up and put on the back of a little flatbed truck. 'And there's your other, three of three.'

Eddie put the third box on the wooden truck as she flicked through her book and found where he had to sign, and then he signed and watched as she tore out his copy, gave it to him and climbed back into the van. He picked up the long metal 'T' of the handle and dragged the wooden truck towards his desk.

Every time she got him to sign the book she held it for him and he could see the outline of her bra through the yellow of the company polo shirt, and how she burst a bit over the cups, and every time she did it she had the same effect on him and must have guessed as much, and he thought that maybe she did the same all day to lots of different men starved of the sight of women in warehouses all over Manchester, and that it perhaps helped her get through the day too.

He kept his finger on the button to close the shutter door and started to get busy with the deliveries, lifted like he was after every time he saw her, and that every time the bell rang made him hope for her, even though it was usually just some little fat bloke stressed out and rushing, or lonely and rambling and keeping the conversation going long after Eddie had got cold and heard enough. He thought briefly of asking the DHL woman's name, but then was aware of the belly that hid his own feet, and the itchy skin that blotched his face, and instead thought of the week after pay day, and the short walk to Three Coins and the first cool pint of bitter, and the ten more after that took him to serene sleep, via Tommy Duck's, beneath the trees and stars on the soft as a bed feeling benches of Piccadilly Gardens.

On the night of his 21st birthday, after he'd turned down his parent's half-hearted offer of a party and not told anyone at work about it, Eddie took part in the annual stock take at the warehouse. It started at 8 p.m. on Friday night and carried on for twelve hours through that night until 8 a.m. on Saturday morning, so as not to affect distribution, and was paid at time and a half, and was referred to as '8 while 8'. For the best part of twelve hours, not including breaks, Eddie counted fixtures and fittings out of wooden lockers into bags before emptying them back into the lockers and tucking a little card behind the label, with a number on it that might be five, or five hundred, or five thousand. And it was when he was counting into the thousands of close taper nipples that he first felt the futility it; first felt that somehow the extra on his pay slip wasn't worth it; first felt the regret that he'd always have of being too shy for a 21st party and not wanting to cause a fuss, until, eventually, he saw the hope of light at five in the morning — the first light shining on his 22nd year — and he wished he was drunk and anywhere but where he was, standing hunched over in navy blue overalls and steel toe-capped boots, with oil blackened hands and sweat cooling under his armpits and on his aching back, counting objects he didn't know the purpose of out of splintered wooden lockers in shady corridors, over cold floors where poison sat in boxes in the corners and the air was damp with cold and rust under a sheet metal roof that kept out the sun and the sky.

When 8 a.m. came and everyone cheered up and the alarm was set and the warehouse door was pad-locked behind them, Eddie made his way through the industrial estate and saw condoms and beer cans on the floor, and a bottle blonde with a fur coat and knee length brown boots getting out of a car, showing a long stretch of pale white, almost light blue, bruised thigh, the back of which wobbled with wrinkles as she adjusted her skirt and stood on the corner and asked Eddie as he passed if he wanted any business. But it was all Eddie could do to make it to the bus stop, where he swayed, aching for the 81 and sleep and the day he saw an affordable Escort in *Exchange & Mart*. And when he did get back on the bus he looked through the window at the woman and despite himself felt the beginnings of lust for her, and felt the sadness and desperation of that and her as he fell asleep and ending up missing his stop, so that he had to pay again when the bus turned around in Oldham town centre. At home he didn't go straight to bed like he wanted to, but instead sat at the kitchen table and ate the bacon butty that his smiling Mum had left under the grill.

Feeling sad at both his memories and the thought of the DHL driver, Eddie switched on the cassette player and put in the *For the Lonely* tape, and sang into the handle of a sweeping brush as one of his favourite songs, 'In Dreams', reverberated around the white painted brick walls of the warehouse: 'A candy-coloured clown they call the sandman, tiptoes to my room every night, just to sprinkle stardust and to whisper, go to sleep, everything is all right.'

A new lad had started, and was going to be helping Eddie in Goods Inward, and he looked a bit bemused as the forty five year old man with the beer belly standing before him swayed around with his sweeping brush.

Eddie could see the lad's bemusement and revelled in the audience, and when 'Oh Pretty Woman' came on he picked up the sweeping brush and held it sideways like a guitar, and pretended to play it as Roy the boy's haunted tones rang out over shrink-wrapped boxes and pallets piled with fixtures and fittings.

The new lad was called Nick, and Eddie saw how rapidly Nick's enthusiasm had begun to fade as he fully realized the nature of the job and how tiring it was. Already Nick had had the piss taken out of him by the other lads because in his tiredness he kept sitting down, and soon enough there was a tell-tale black mark on the arse of his otherwise clean new overalls that showed him to be lazy, and maybe weak, and maybe not up to the work.

Eddie showed him what to do with delivery notes and invoices, and how to use a pump truck, and whereabouts in the warehouse particular fixtures and fittings had to go. He took him upstairs and showed him the idiosyncrasies of the goods lift that could keep you imprisoned for hours at a time, but that if you felt like a rest gave you the perfect excuse.

Nick took it all in pretty quickly and Eddie thought about the job he was doing that could be easily learned in a matter of days, and was only surprised that it took so long for Nick to leave. He said he was going to University, and Eddie wished he'd done something similar when he was young enough, but with the hard work and the boozing and the family to keep he'd not even considered it before. He knew too late that the best jobs, and more importantly the *best paid* jobs, were the ones where you used your brain, and that the job you had would always sum you up to people, right or wrong.

When he'd moved out of the office and into the warehouse the idea of physical work appealed to Eddie more than being cooped up behind a desk waiting for the telephone to ring, or talking on that telephone to people who'd never have the bravery to talk to him like that in person. But now, in his forty sixth year, with big sloping shoulders and strong arms still, a permanent niggle in his back, a cantankerous ulcer and an occasionally aching liver, he sometimes thought of how his life might have been, working in a job where he wasn't physically knackered every night and that dulled his brain's reactions with fatigue and under-use, and where he still had the energy to do more than just go to the pub and drink deeply, feeling a pleasure in and reliance upon the refreshment of booze that only men who work with their hands can really know.

During the second year, when sleep was even more troubled than in the first, he looked at the thin line of light under his door and remembered a school trip to the Peak District, and seeing a man with a border collie seemingly floating across the heather, and thinking to himself how that would be a great way to be. That youthful day in summer, on a weekday in Edale, with nobody around save a gang of schoolmates and Mr Miller, they'd got off the train and into the landscape that had emerged and risen from the windows in the minutes before, among green hills beneath blue skies marked by fading vapour trails. They walked through the village and up Grindsbrook, following the stream that started in a gush and turned into sparkling trickles

117

until they reached the top of the climb and a plateau of dried black peat and thick heather. He could see all around to Oldham and Manchester, and Derbyshire, and he remembered aeroplanes that seemed so low, and as they walked along the spongy peat filled with overlapping footprints he listened to all the birdsong and looked down at the white flowers around his feet that shook so slightly in the freshening breeze. He saw hares springing among their camouflage, and grouse rustling away through the heather, and birds swooping and rising and teasing in a tiny air show all around them; and as he lay on his bed he thought that he should go again; get the train back there, if only to confirm such dreams of freedom and youth.

It was the accident that gave Eddie another and bigger reason for his drinking. It had been a long time ago now, and only Keith Taylor, who was still foreman, remained from those years before. It was the accident that meant he no longer drove the forklift; and the accident that meant he lost his driving licence and spent two and a half years inside; and that left him so fearful of getting behind a wheel he'd never driven a car again.

It was that first week after pay day, and, as was his habit at the time, Eddie had a few pints of bitter after work before driving his battered Ford Escort home, having something to eat with Mary and then going back out without the car to his local. That particular night he decided to drive home a slightly different way than usual, to avoid the extra traffic in town caused by a European game at Eastlands.

The white blur bounced up off the front of the car

and into the windscreen before him, which cracked, and he watched the football flung into the air from the boy's hands. He pulled the handbrake on and put the gears into neutral and switched off the engine and left the car where it was, in the middle of the road, barely five yards from the body. A boy racer came speeding up behind and revved his engine and beeped his horn for Eddie to move the car, somehow not seeing. And Eddie remembered the screaming woman, and the man who punched him into bushes; and he remembered sitting dazed among those bushes until the police came and told him to blow through a straw.

When he came out to graffiti on his house, and dog shit and worse dropped through his letterbox, it took him a further few months of abuse before finally Eddie and his family were able to move to a town where his picture in the local paper had been less memorable, and where most if not all people just saw him as a bloke in his twenties, with a wife, who didn't have a car and so caught the bus to work. And as the years passed only Keith Taylor remained from that time and never said anything to anybody about how and why Eddie got his job back.

II

Kevin Whitley had been unemployed since losing his job at a bakery outside Oldham, and had long since stopped having to get up in the small hours to drive through dark silent streets to Park Cakes. The people at the dole office sent him on adult literacy courses, but he just sat there looking at the jumbles on the white board and getting lost in the nervous words of the tutors.

Once, when he'd put his head down on the desk in exasperation, the bloke with thinning hair and beads around his neck and black denims on standing at the front told him to read some of the words on the board, and when he laughed and was nervous and couldn't, the tutor made him try not once, not twice, but three times to read the words out. And so for the next few Tuesday afternoons Kevin sat attentively in his chair, entirely co-operative and learning nothing.

He lived in what the Housing Association called a maisonette. It backed onto a canal, and sometimes he would sit in the yard with a fishing line thrown over the fence. In summer he could see when barges were coming because of the ripples that preceded them, and he'd frown at the people on those barges—most often old couples, sometimes with a little dog—as he lifted his line out of the water.

For the last ten years his only intimacies had been on holiday in Thailand, and the last time he'd gone he'd been close to bringing a girl back with him. She was called Theva and he met her in Bangkok and she cost him 500 baht a night. He'd seen her first on the stage, where she put razor blades inside herself and took them out again, and magic markers that she took back out and drew childish pictures with. She emptied a bottle of milk inside herself and then put the bottle in too, and looked right into his eyes as she did it. He knew it was crazy but he had the money, and the first night he took her back to his hotel she went down on him like nobody had before, and made so much noise and made herself available in so many different ways, and was so intense, that when he sobered up he was a bit scared, at least until the end of the next night's show when he waited for her again, emboldened by a dozen tequilas.

On the last night of his holiday they had unprotected sex. She asked him for his home telephone number, and suggested that she come to England, and he remembered everything during the flight home and felt disgusted. But for all that, when he lay in his own bed alone with his hands on only himself, he still wished he had the money to go back to Thailand.

Now his mind was opened up to the things that Theva did, he started looking for them again in the privacy of his bedroom. The broadband connection had come in a cheap package with the TV and telephone, and through it he could find women who would remind him of Theva but didn't want his money or a visa. He looked at many different websites that catered to a variety of tastes, and soon he was filling the base of a coffee mug thanks to all kinds of women; and one in particular called Camilla Lopez, and he watched her so much and on so many different websites that even his dreams began to contain her, and he saw himself doing to her what he'd only ever seen other men and women doing on a screen. On the street, or in a shop, he began to look at every woman as though she were performing a sex act, looking particularly at her lips and thinking of what he had to put there.

With a limited amount of money to last him every fortnight he couldn't afford to go out much. When he'd been out with the one or two friends he'd known from Park Cakes it was obvious that now they didn't work together they no longer had that in common, and so after a few old jokes the conversation died. And when one of the lads phoned up again, Kevin thought of how little money he had and said no to the invitation, and just went to the off licence for four cans of lager.

Awake in bed because he'd done nothing to make himself tired, one day in particular kept returning to his mind, and he began to see it as the day that had led into all his others. It seemed to him as though he could remember exactly what had happened.

'Come over here, I want to show you something,' said the foreman. 'Now I know we've been having a bit of a laugh with you this morning, but we need you to have a look at this shopping trolley you were using before.'

'This isn't another wind up is it?'

'No, no. Look, Eddie says there's something wrong with one of the wheels.'

Kevin bent over to look, and when he did so, Eddie and Tony grabbed his back legs. He fought against them, but then Nick and Keith joined in too, and he stopped kicking like a struggling pet and subsided as though injected, trying and failing to smile as Tony picked up a tape gun and went round and round the trolley with it, and Eddie loosened a ball of string and fastened that round his waist, and across the top of the trolley and right round and under it, tighter and tighter so that he felt it on his ribs, and then they stuck the yellow cone on his head, and taped his mouth and with a marker pen drew a moustache on the tape and a beard on his face, before finally Eddie wheeled him out behind the trade counter, where Kevin sat watching as the queue of men, young and old, laughed and laughed, until finally, one of the company directors heard the noise from the office and came out and laughed briefly too, before wheeling Kevin back into the warehouse and, stifling a smirk, telling Keith to get Kevin out of the trolley.

Tony and Eddie were still laughing as they got knives and cut away the tape and the string, and Kevin pushed them away and struggled out of the trolley on his own, tipping it over before standing up.

'He looks like one of those Amish fuckers!' said Keith, pointing to Kevin's face, and everyone cracked up again.

In the toilet, Kevin scrubbed and scrubbed, using Swarfega and hot water, and his cheeks were red and dripping by the time he got most of the marker pen off. That afternoon he felt like people were laughing at him still, even people who'd only heard about it in the office and who came out to smoke and to snigger.

That night, at home in his bedroom, in his parents' house, he did press ups on the floor until he was exhausted and went to bed planning a defiant return the next day. But when he got up in the morning, to the sound of the alarm in the dark, his first thoughts were of the laughter, and his stomach sank and he lost any conviction the press ups had given him, and when his mum came in thinking he'd slept through the alarm he told her he was ill, and listened to her unquestioning sympathy and the muffled argument she had with his dad, before his dad went off to work.

He remembered seeing the picture in the paper and connecting it immediately to that workplace, and now it seemed like something he could do; something he

123

might be capable of; something that might redress a kind of imbalance.

Careless of his lack of insurance and tax, he put a few quid in the petrol tank of his car and drove into town before rush hour, parking up on a side street of the industrial estate. He didn't quite know what he was doing there, but he did know that he wasn't interested in the hookers who lingered, shivering in the glow of streetlights.

After the first week he put a few more quid in the tank and spent another week watching the door of the warehouse. He saw the fat man, who all the first week had gone straight to the bus stop. Now the man was going to the pub first instead, and he realized the bastard was still drinking. With his hands sometimes whitening on the wheel, he waited and then watched as an hour or so later the fat man crossed over the road to the bus stop. *It must be him*, Kevin thought. It would be too much of a coincidence for it not to be; he must have just been losing his hair; put on weight, grown a lot older.

Rain covered the windscreen, and he flicked the wipers when he could no longer see through the spots. It was dark, and had been for most of the day; was like that most days now. The workers came out in the same order every night, never noticing him as they rushed into their cars, or off to the train station or bus stop. And almost to the second, there he was, the old bastard, waddling past the pub as he'd hoped. Kevin started the car and drove it to the junction near the bus stop, and when the fat man started to cross over he put his foot down and swung left onto the main road, where he was crashed into from behind and sent across the chevrons into the line of oncoming traffic, one car of which hit him side on and spiralling into a brick wall next to a betting shop.

He opened his eyes to see the roof of the car inches from his face and drifted in and out of consciousness as the firemen cut him from the wreckage. When he was lifted into the ambulance by the paramedics he saw the bus stop where the queue had been.

It was the middle of the night, and as a result of a combination of painkillers he was feeling both drowsy and ill at ease. His neck was still in a brace, and in front of him were motionless lumps of bodies under white sheets. When the nurse came she stopped and picked up his bedpan.

'Is everything all right, Kevin?' she asked, softly.

'Yeah, fine.'

'Are you sure?' Let's have a little look.'

She pulled back the sheets and looked down without disgust. Kevin was brought more fully to consciousness by his embarrassment and could only sit there as, smiling, she quietly slid away the spoiled white of the bedclothes and clothing and he waited on the moonlit ward as she came back with clean replacements.

When he left he waved to the nurse on his way out, but she just busied herself with another patient. He smiled to himself as he walked into the cold air that showed him his breathing, and then considered for a moment before getting into a taxi.

A few weeks after returning home, when the silence of

his rooms became louder than the fear of leaving them, he had a few beers in Oldham before getting on the 81.

'So who's Tommy Duck?' he said to the barman, a wiry man with jam jar glasses and smudged blue tattoos on both arms.

'If I had a quid for every time someone asked me that.'

'Sorry.'

'They reckon that when some bloke came to do the sign there wasn't enough room to paint Tommy Duckworth's, so it ended up as Tommy Duck's.'

'Oh right. That's all there is to it.'

'Afraid so. That's all I was told anyway.'

'Well, cheers, now I know. I'll have another one.'

'Another Carling?'

'Yeah.'

It was near closing time when the old man turned up, swaying and glassy eyed. He stood next to where Kevin leaned on the bar, beneath the collection of yellowed knickers hanging from the ceiling, and asked the barman with the jam jar glasses for a drink.

'I was thinking you weren't coming,' said the barman, but before the old man could get his wits together enough to reply, Kevin said, 'I'll get these. And I'll have another Carling, cheers.'

The old man thanked him and sat down in the corner on his own, at a table that was glass on top of a coffin, and with his face lit by the glow of the television. At closing time he got up and waved goodbye to the barman, and Kevin followed him out as the door was locked behind them.

Kevin didn't feel the cold as he walked towards the centre of town through a trail of fading footprints.

There was only a small queue at the taxi rank so he didn't have to wait long, and after wiping condensation from the window of the moving cab, he saw the old man, shuffling towards Piccadilly Gardens, slowly disappearing in the snowfall.

BAR

I go in this bar in town on Monday nights. I sit on my own and drink and don't talk to anyone. There's this Bukowski poem where he's at the racetrack and somebody comes over to sit next to him and Bukowski gets up and walks a hundred yards away and sits down again. I've always liked that poem.

There's a bouncer on the door in this bar. Not always the same one. Bouncers come and go like confidence. The difference is that they have to be there and I don't. Same with the barmaids, they are often different too. You see I don't go in every week. I go maybe once a month. But to them I am that way all the time. There are bouncers and barmaids who understand drinking and there are bouncers and barmaids who don't. Barmaids come and go too and when they go it is like innocence. One girl is still there though. She's been on about leaving for years.

One time I went in this other place and there was this new barmaid, well someone I hadn't seen before anyway. And she was doing that thing that women do when they want to get your attention—talking to someone close by about things they think might interest you. And because I was there to drink and not talk to anyone I ignored her, and because I ignored her she became more interested. She was talking to this bloke on the stool next to me, when she could get a word in.

He was going on about his band and how they were hoping to make it big and how he had been drinking whisky since early that morning. Now when you drink at a bar it doesn't matter how much you ignore people, you can't help being aware of what is going on either side of you, and this bloke hadn't touched his drink since coming in.

Some guys come in the bar and talk to me because they somehow see that I am wise; see that I know the folly of ambition and am philosophical enough to just sit at a bar and watch the world go by. Women don't see that so much, and only now and then do they come and talk and usually that's to get a drink. But this barmaid wasn't after a drink from me, why would she be? She was excited by her new job, thought she was going to meet some characters. Barmaids always start that way.

All the time this guy was talking to her I could tell she kept looking at me. Then she started saying things she thought I might like to hear, about how real drinkers don't talk about how much they drink and how some men are comfortable not talking at all, and how what she really liked in a man was someone who would listen. Then when I kept ignoring her (and him) she said that some men were quiet because they didn't have anything to say, and that any idiot could look wise if he didn't say anything. And she said that some men didn't talk because they were shy. She really didn't know when to stop talking. And the more she said the more I ignored her. Late on in the evening, just before the ten minutes fast clock ticked to one, she stood right opposite me on the other side of the bar so I couldn't ignore her any more. She rested her little

T-shirted breasts on the bar, one of them touching my right hand that held the beer. She looked right into my eyes. I noticed then how much make up she had on. She said she was thinking about staying after work for a drink and I ignored her. Then she said she didn't know where she was going to stay after. She revolted me and I told her to leave me alone.

I had a bit of money around that time and I was in town the next day and ended up in the bar again. And it's true if you drink a lot one night you can drink whatever you want the next day and not get drunk. So from early afternoon I drank my way across town, moving from pubs and bars the whole way and never talking to anyone except to ask for a drink. In pubs and bars where people don't know you it's best to just stay for one drink and then move on, more than that and you can see them getting uneasy. Sometimes if I want to stay in a place for more than one then that's when I'll talk, say something banal to the barman or barmaid just so they realize I'm not crazy. Most of these people have never read Bukowski. Most people don't see a man who chooses to be alone; they just see an absence of friends.

I had no idea that this barmaid was going to be working again. I had completely forgotten about her. And she wasn't working when I first went in the bar. But somehow the other barmaids seemed even less welcoming than the day before. At the change of shift she came behind the bar to start work and she was quiet, sullen, not talking to anyone more than she had to. And she was all covered up with a big sweater. She kept looking at my drink so that when I was getting to the end of the bottle she knew not to catch my eye. I thought how stupid it was that she could be so affected by someone she didn't even know. And then I thought well, of course it's nothing to do with me. That's a thing with not talking to anyone and drinking on your own, sometimes you end up thinking that everything is about you and a lot of the time it isn't. You can be over-attentive to your surroundings.

Later on she rolled up her sleeves as if to emphasise the point. That night the other barmaid took my unfinished bottle away after I got up to go to the toilet and at the end of the night the bouncer was aggressive and wouldn't let me finish my drink. Bouncers can be like that sometimes; especially if there's only you left in the bar and they've been waiting.

The sad thing is that most people just can't be alone, they get lonely. When I go out to the bar it's not to meet people, it's to get out of my flat. And once, maybe twice per month I go out and have a drink. I'm not doing anyone any harm. If people want to harm themselves then it's nothing to do with me. They don't let me into that other bar anymore, but there are plenty of pubs and bars in town where I can go for a drink. It doesn't really matter which one it is, just so long as I can get a drink and be left alone. I go in this place now and they know I don't want to talk, and at first they weren't very friendly, but when they realized how much money I was spending they were fine. If you sit at a bar the whole world comes to you in the end.

ROOM

Imagine the room: it smells of body odour, the thin curtains on the big bay windows won't draw together, the reflection of the streetlight shines in on the dirty white wallpaper and the rest is lit by a low wattage bulb. The brown carpet curls at the corners and holds trails of tumbled plaster, the dark blue couch sags and is scarred by burns. There are battered guitar cases and battered guitars, a keyboard overhanging an armchair, amps covered in cup rings. Bookcases — home-made — fill the alcoves and hold science fiction, science, music biogs and an eclectic mix of fiction ranging from Burroughs through Ballard to bestsellers. *Zen and the Art of Motorcycle Maintenance* has a cracked spine.

He stays there after drinking in town because it's too late to get back to the country. The biscuit tin on the coffee table is never empty and when he gets back to the room he rolls a joint to help him sleep. If that doesn't do it he has a few sips from his hip flask. She is in a secure unit close by.

There is something about the woman you love that doesn't fit in with what you think you most like about women. This is thanks to media and inexperience. Magic knew when he met Stacey at school but only realized until a couple of years after finding things out with others. In the schoolroom they used to sit oppo-site each other and kick each other's shins under the table. After school he started as a builder's mate and ended up with his own roofing business. She got a job in the sweet factory that backed onto the canal and he met her one Friday night after a gig. She had two kids and was paying for a sitter. She was full of love and a lot knew it already, but when she met Magic it was like they'd been saving themselves up for each other, and neither could ever see Tyler and Jordan as mistakes.

They lived in a terraced house with a cellar near the canal in Furness Vale. They had no time for politics, no time for anything beyond the immediate concerns of family. Magic had the monopoly on building work in a part of the Peak where word of mouth means more than advertising. But the father of her children never went from her mind and Stacey got careless in a drinking way. Magic could never get over the beauty of her nose. It had been broken by a hockey stick at school but he only noticed the bump when he stroked it with his finger.

He got the nickname Magic because when he was a kid he was always disappearing. And when he got older the name was great for business. But somehow he couldn't be magic for Stacey. He was great with the kids and looked after them when he could so she could go out with her mates, but she kept telling him he worked too much.

They were sitting in the living room together, the stone walls of the terrace and the little light through the windows keeping the room cool even on a hot summer day.

'Mage, I don't ever see you,' she said.

'I'm working, sweetheart. I have to take it when it comes.'

'People round here are always going to need stuff doing. What about us, what about me and you?'

'Look, do you have to work? No, so I work. I pay for the food; I pay for your wine.'

'It's always that, isn't it? It always comes back to that. What about you, what about your beer?'

'If you'd been on a roof all day you would know what it is to be thirsty.'

'And if you had been looking after Tyler and Jord you would know that I have to work hard too.'

'Well I'm not complaining about that.'

'Well I don't think you realize how hard that is.'

'I know, sweetheart, I'm sorry. I'm sorry. Come here.'

'I don't know why I put up with you.'

'Yes you do.'

'You are a pain in the arse.'

'Come here,' he said, and they sat closer on the couch and kissed.

They drank more and more, and as Magic could take it he kept up. But soon he was beginning to feel the effects in the morning. Because he was with her every night and because he was drinking for a long time he didn't notice the changes. She had always been lively and livelier after a drink and the basis of their love had always been physical, but one night she threatened to break his neck.

'Why don't you kiss me anymore?' she said, the next night.

'What?'

'Why don't you fucking kiss me anymore? We just have sex.'

'That's not true.'

'Of course it is and you know it. In fact we don't even have sex. I go down on you and that's it.'

'You're talking out of your arse, love.'

'Fuck you. Don't ever talk to me like that.'

'Shut up, you'll wake the kids.'

'Don't tell me to shut up.'

'You're pissed.'

'I am not pissed. I've only had two bottles.'

'Have you heard yourself? *I've only had two bottles.* Don't you think two bottles is enough?'

'You don't love me.'

'What are you going on about now? How do you go from me talking about drinking to *you don't love me*?'

'You don't.'

'You're pissed.'

'Fuck off!' she shouted.

'Jesus Christ, Stacey. I'm going to bed. There's plenty more wine in there,' he said, pointing to the kitchen then starting upstairs.

'Fine, fine. Go to bed, you fucking loser.'

In bed he watched his chest falling and rising under the sheets. He thought of how he worked so hard for her and the kids he loved like his own. He stayed awake, the voices from TV distracting and indiscernible, and only relaxed when he thought she'd passed out.

Magic met Alison when he put a Velux window in her roof. It was the middle of a hot spell in summer and he was working shirtless in the sun by himself. After several cups of tea that prolonged the job she offered him a beer. He sat on the extra lawn chair she brought out and put next to hers. This was in Marple, in a house that backed onto the canal locks. Her lawn ran straight down to the water's edge and her garden had no fences. They sat and watched the barges slowly rising or falling. She mentioned before he left that she was thinking of a kitchen extension.

They bonded while he did it and though she wasn't sure about the lessening of the lawn it was a warmer place to sit in the evenings. She told him sadly of her divorce and happily of her work as a family solicitor in Marple, but mostly she got him to talk about himself, and gradually he confided more. And then one day with the blinds closed and windows shut and the mid-summer sun still shining in through the early evening windows, she unfastened her bra and brought his head to her breasts with love.

Leaving Stacey and the kids gave him a bad name in Furness Vale, where most people knew the facts and not the details. And though he moved away from the Peak and away from Marple with Alison to a place in the country a train ride away from anywhere he knew, Stacey made him aware of her decline. And when his conscience could no longer keep him away he went to see her. This was long after they'd taken Tyler and Jordan and long after the last of the hospitalisations. And she was around the corner from a room he knew. She looked at him with all the anger gone and most of all the life gone and she was nice to him.

FLAT

I magine the flat: part of a building painted green, with a green door and the number 63 screwed on in gold letters. Cobwebs cross the letters from the bricks near the door; the door itself has a black film on it caused by the traffic on the Mancunian Way. The windowsill below the kitchen window has a thicker layer of film, and you can write your name in the dust on the windows. It is six floors up. You can see Eastlands from the kitchen window and before that trains going in and out from Piccadilly. If you are on a train you can see the flats as the building painted green behind an almost identical building painted blue. Inside the door you step onto a black lino floor. Above you there is a hole in the ceiling caused by damp, and from where, during thunderstorms, water falls and brings down wet plaster that plops on the black floor. The white wooden door that leads into the living room is black around the grey handle, and needs a solid push because it sticks. In the living room a big grey rug covered in stains and dust fills most of the black floor. A glass coffee table with a thick layer of dust sits on top of the rug. In the corner there is a big silver TV on the floor. The couch is grey with a faint whiff of come. Under the cushions there is a layer of washing powder to lessen the smell. On the white ceiling above there is a stain of damp resembling a flattened sunflower. Wind blows in through gaps in the closed white window frames. The white radiators give off a dry heat partly negated by the draft. On the windowsill under the windows a table lamp with a scorched lampshade gives off an expanding triangle of white light. In the bedroom there is a double mattress on the floor covered by a black duvet. On the floor beside the mattress there is an ashtray, a lighter, a packet of cigarettes and a mobile. A big black wardrobe half covers the window on which there are no curtains. Like the windows from the living room the view at night is that of streetlights and the moving headlights of cars. There is a pedestrian crossing and from the window you can see the red man and the green man. In the bathroom there is a dirty enamel bath and sink, above which is a cabinet filled with tablets. The mirror on the cabinet is smudged where a hand has wiped away condensation. Below the window there is a large red towel sitting in the dust on the black lino floor. From the bath to the door there is a walkway through the dust. In the toilet there is an empty bit of plastic that held a urinal cake. The water in the toilet is black.

Kirsty is still in bed. She's woken by a wolf whistle from below. The lamp in the living room has been on all day. It is dark again now. She reaches for the mobile then a cigarette. There's a message on the phone from Keano. She gets up off the mattress and looks out of the window. He is looking up at her from a car in the car park. A young lad, tall, gets out of the back of the car and walks across the car park. When he knocks she lets him in. He smells of vodka. From the way he talks she guesses he is Polish.

Along the Mancunian Way the traffic is sporadic compared to the daytime. There are lorry's, often Eddie Stobart ones or Royal Mail ones, some fast cars, and motorbikes disturbing the relative repose of the wind in the trees. On the road into town the occasional car stops at the traffic lights. A billboard turns around at intervals, a different advertisement either side. At the back of a derelict building next to the flats a rat explores inside a ripped bin liner. The streetlight shines on broken glass beside an abandoned car. Another car is parked by the kerb on Grosvenor Street. The window on the passenger's side is smashed.

The Polish lad leaves. Kirsty goes to the bathroom and then down to Keano in the car.

'Alright?' he asks.

'Yeah.'

'Right, well. Let's go,' he says, swinging the car out of the car park. They turn right and then right again at the lights, under the Mancunian Way and back round past UMIST, past the Alan Turing sculpture in the park near Canal Street and across London Road to Fairfield Street. He drops her off outside The Star and Garter, and as it's raining she walks a bit further up Fairfield Street to stand in the streetlight under the railway bridge. She's wearing a mini skirt and black boots that reach above her knees. She folds her arms across her chest to keep warm. After two the taxis increase, taking people home from town to the suburbs. When that rush subsides the stragglers come. She can see them a mile away. She sees him walking down Fairfield Street in a wavering line, a wavering line that sometimes drops him off the kerb into a brief stagger on the road. He is smartly dressed in dark jacket and trousers, but his white shirt is hanging out. Near the Star and Garter he throws a packet of condoms high into the air and they land and spill out under the orange of the streetlights. She waits. He doesn't see her until a couple of yards away and then his head lifts back from looking at the ground. When she asks, 'Any business love?' she can tell at first he doesn't know what she means. This is a good sign. She can guess he won't get aggressive, though she's been wrong about that before. She takes him by the hand and walks him back for the condoms. Then she leads him into the industrial area just up from The Star and Garter. All the time he is trying to say it's not a good idea. Then she feels him. Under the railway arches, beyond the view of cameras and behind a stack of pallets, where ripped shrink wrap flickers above black puddles and everything smells of wood and oil, she asks him for the money first. He protests in a weak way and then gives it her: a fiver and a heavy pile of pound coins and smaller change. She puts it all in her handbag and then starts walking away. He grabs her and she starts to scream. As soon as she screams he lets her go. She walks back up to the Star and Garter. She can hear him shouting and then sees him kicking at the bricks of the railway arch. She watches as he runs down the road towards the suburbs.

Kirsty is cold when Keano turns up. He laughs and says she can't get in, but then relents and lets her sit in the passenger seat beside him. It is very warm in the car. She feels the life return to her hands warmed only between two fingers by a cigarette. He rubs his hand on her cold thighs, touches her between them. He presses the button that lowers his window, collects phlegm in his throat and spits. She hears the spit land on the road.

Two men turn the corner and walk past the line of cabs outside Piccadilly Station. Keano pushes her out of the car and she is waiting with her question as they pass. The two men laugh at her. Keano watches from the car and grips the steering wheel harder. He looks at her under the streetlight. She has frizzy bleached blonde hair and he's sick of her. She wears the same clothes every day. He has better girls than her now. He loosens his hands on the wheel and drives away, the tyres spinning through the changing lights.

In the centre of town, a man high up in an office block watches a bank of screens. He sees the girl with the frizzy blonde hair walking up and down Fairfield Street. Sometimes he doesn't see her for a few months at a time but she always comes back. He knows that hair and those boots and soon he will try to find her. Most of the time he is busy watching other things, usually fighting in the city centre or men urinating on Market Street in full view. And though the cameras cover more and more every year, Kirsty knows the places she can't be seen. She knows she will be seen leading the man there and that and Keano and the stuff she takes off him are just enough to stop her thinking of things like being under the arches on the night of her sixteenth birthday.

As the darkness turns gradually to the dull winter light of a wet Manchester morning, and the traffic volume increases hour after hour until peaking, she puts her fob to the door, goes up six floors in the silver coffin of the lift and returns to the flat. There is something broken in the meter and she gets heating and hot water for free. By turning on the taps she covers the hum of traffic on the Mancunian Way. She drags off her boots and takes off her clothes and steps into the hot bath. She lowers herself in, likes it as hot as she can stand so it reddens her naked body. There is a withered cake of soap still damp from the night before. She rubs it to a lather and washes herself in cursory swipes. That out of the way, she lies there in the deep, hot water.

SUN ON PROSPECT STREET

Their house is opposite a glue factory and they grow up knowing the smell of melting horses. Behind the house the motorway runs in a constant raised drone, slicing through what once was a village. Parallel to the motorway, on the other side, is the canal that once carried limestone barges, parallel to that, the railway that still carries limestone.

By the side of the railway there is a football pitch with leaning over goalposts and a long line of trampled grass through the middle leading to mud in the penalty areas. Crows inspect the mud and complain about the noise from the motorway. The canal where balls are sometimes lost is floated on by ducks and geese and sometimes the diluted rainbows of fuel. The odd lone figure sits on the bank smoking and drinking lager by a long motionless rod dipped into the flat water. The other side of the canal bank is filled with rustling and cracking reeds. In the evening the branches of tall trees shadow a braided fringe across the water.

The canal leads under the arches of the motorway bridge, and they sit under it, at the precipice of a sloping concrete bank stained where water pours down it on rainy days and lessens the spray in the lanes above. Sometimes they graffiti the concrete canvas. One big painted swirl reads the legend *Baggers*. Smaller comments in marker pen surround it: *is a dick* being one.

143

They eat crisps and drink cans of pop and wedge the cans and crisp packets in gaps in the concrete when they've finished. Above the reeds on the other side of the bank there is a field where a white horse drinks from a bathtub. When it rains the horse walks across the boggy field and stands under the motorway bridge. Geese float along the canal and under the bridge too, though ducks stay out among a million holes.

The summer holidays they waited so long for have becoming boring after only one week. Five more weeks seem to stretch out forever. They sit under the muted roar of the motorway. Joe flicks through the creased magazine that also curls up at either side from being rolled. He looks at the picture: a topless woman in a shower, foam covering her breasts. He looks through the rest of the magazine and passes it to Leo before asking, 'Have you got any pubes yet?'

Leo takes the magazine first then puts it down on the concrete by his side, where it curls up again. 'I'll have a look,' he says, holding out his tracksuit bottoms. 'Three. I've got three.'

'I've got more than that,' says Joe. Just then a man walks along the towpath below them at the bottom of the concrete slope. He is watching as his black dog threatens to jump in the canal after the ducks. Leo shouts, 'I've got three pubes!' and the man turns round and looks up to where they sit. Unimpressed, he walks on. Finally the dog plunges into the water and the ducks flap and crash away and the man has to drag his dog out, the fur all slick and heavy, dripping wet patterns on the path.

Joe looks at Leo and then at the magazine and Leo picks the magazine up and looks through it. Joe keeps looking down at the water. Sometimes a jogger passes along the path, then a man at the back of a barge. A sign painted on the wooden side of the barge spells *Desperado* and the man is wearing a cowboy hat. He sees them but avoids eye contact and instead stares out at the slow miles of canal ahead. A woman sits under a dark blue parasol at the other end of the barge. 'I'm going for my dinner,' says Joe, and Leo rolls up the magazine, stashes it behind a pillar and follows him down the back path to Prospect Street.

In the afternoon they go to the football pitch with Leo's ball. It's a Mitre casey they fished out of the canal the week before, when Leo fell in. The ball is white with little 'v' shapes all over it. They had to pump it up a bit with an adapter and a bicycle pump. If they kicked at goal from outside the area they would barely reach. And standing in the goal mouth Leo looks like he'll always be too tiny for a keeper. There's no netting in the goals so Leo has to run for the ball every time Joe scores and every time Joe hits it wide or over Joe has to go for it. After a while they play headers and volleys, Joe or Leo crossing from the side for one or the other to head or volley towards the empty goal. Both end up with mud on their heads. At one point Leo steps in some dog muck and spends an age wiping it off, twisting his ankle to slide his trainers on the grass. Joe is tired and so goes over and leans against a goal post, then sits down against it and wipes the sweat from his head, covering his hand with the dried mud off it. There's mud all over his trainers and on the inside right leg of his tracksuit bottoms. The afternoon sun is shining warm across the football pitch, glints on the canal and dazzles on vehicles whistling past on the motorway. It sinks across the chimneys of the terraced houses colouring the bricks red rose.

Leo wanders over, kicking the ball. 'There's none on the ball is there?' asks Joe.

'No.'

'What about on your trainers?'

'No, look,' he says, lifting up his leg and turning the underside of his shoe so Joe can see.

Leo sits down on the ball next to Joe. A crow lands in the mud in the opposite goalmouth and pecks at the ground before leaning back to croak at them.

'When are you moving?' asks Leo.

'Next week I think.'

There's a row of big houses along the main road into town. The houses back onto a railway line then reservoirs. Starting at one end they dart across lawns, duck under washing lines, scoot across patios, leave footsteps in flower beds, wobble over creosoted fences, send cats running, dogs barking and are pursued all the way by their shadows running sideways on the ground. At the end of the row they run over the railway lines and up onto the reservoirs, where the water shines vast and silver and spreads out before them as they climb the bank and look over the low stone wall.

'Do you think we could swim across there?' asks Leo.

'Don't be daft. We'd probably drown,' answers Joe.

'It's not that far.'

'Well I'm not doing it. What time do you have to be in?'

Leo looked at his watch. 'Oh shit, I'm too late already.'

Joe takes another look at the water, the ripples in the light wind a moving corrugation in the moonlight. They run down the grassy slope beside the stone steps, climb back over the wall again and follow the old farm track back to the road where the chevrons are lit by the orange of the streetlights and cars sometimes pass. A couple walk back from the pub, the woman's legs more wobbly than the man's so that she clings to his arm for support as well as love. On the distant motor-way, lorry's and cars and sometimes motorbikes flash past.

In the morning Leo comes running down the street rebounding the football off walls, bang bang bang and crashing it into rattling metal gates, dribbling around cars, sometimes doing one — two's off their tyres, sending cats running out from under those cars and hackles rising over breakfasts.

Leo calls for Joe, climbing over the fence at the back, walking through the garden and knocking on the back door. Joe shouts him to come in and when he's finished his bowl of cereals Joe gets up and walks in his socks to the back door where he picks up his muddy trainers, puts them on and then takes the ball off Leo.

They walk together to the railway bridge and look through the metal grate at the straight lines stretching out as far as the brick bridge over the main road. The sunlight shines on the lines outside the tunnel and show its curve to the left. Goldfinches flash over embank-ment brambles. Turning around and looking through the metal grate of the bridge in the other direction, they see the straight lines running to another brick bridge, where a lad called Wayne had fallen off and ended up in a wheelchair. From the elevation of the railway bridge they can see the canal and the motorway and the railway line, and the row of houses where they'd been garden creeping and beyond that the walls around the reservoir. They can smell the boiling bones in the glue factory. The fields across the bridge seem to stretch out for miles and they can see the distant hills in the summer sunlight. The fields are empty save for crows and one man walking a brown greyhound. Joe throws the football off the end of the metal bridge and onto the field and they run down the wooden steps after it. 'Bagsy not in net!' shouts Joe and Leo reluctantly kicks the ball to Joe and makes his way between the posts, where he stays until Joe hits one wide and they have to change around because that's the rule.

After they've been playing a while they can hear a distant cracking noise and something that seems to whistle in the grass beside them. It is only when Leo gets hit in the leg that they realize that someone is shooting pellets at them with an air gun. Then three lads are standing by the goalposts and watching.

'How's your leg,' one of them says to Leo, before giggling and not listening for an answer. Leo sits in the grass, rubbing the little red bump on his shin.

The three lads are all taller and the tallest of them starts punching Leo on the arm. Leo backs away and looks down at the floor and seems like he wants to cry. None of the lads approach Joe and he watches as it unfolds. Leo doesn't fight back and so eventually all three of the taller lads are punching him on the arms and kicking him in the shins. Leo stands there and takes it and Joe watches, and then eventually one of the taller lads punches Leo in the face and Leo finally starts crying and the three taller lads run off laughing across the fields.

Leo sits on the grass wiping his eyes and then returns to rubbing his leg where the pellet hit. His face is all red from crying. Joe stands over the football looking at him.

'What are you looking at?' says Leo.

'Nothing,' says Joe. 'Who were they?' he asks, but Leo doesn't answer or even look up from the shin he is rubbing.

'I want my ball back,' says Leo.

'It's not yours,' says Joe, and kicks it in his direction before walking towards home over the railway bridge. On the bridge he stops and looks back and Leo is just gazing down at the grass and not moving.

The next week Joe watches from his bedroom window as a removal man helps Leo's mum and dad put furniture into a big white van. Leo comes out carrying a duvet and a bedside lamp. The van blocks the road and a car that wants to get through is stopped and has to turn around and go back the other way. It takes them a long time to load up the van. Eventually Joe sees the white van pull away, Leo and his parents following in the car behind. He looks at the back of Leo's head until the car turns right at the end of Prospect Street.

EVENING WIND

The house overlooks the bay and an island inhab-
ited by monks. A large green hill dwarfs the
chalk stick of a lighthouse beneath it. The bay itself
is absent of boats since a fishing ban. The coast road
holds a Co-op and a few struggling pubs and B&B's
and curves around the perimeter of the island. The
only other road crosses the island's middle like a ladies
belt. From the top of the mountain at the back of the
house the ferry from the mainland is about the size of
a thumb and doesn't seem to move though it's followed by a lengthening line in the water. From the
mountain top on a clear day you can see the mainland and two other countries as well as the wire of
the coastline road, and because of that road the island
never quite seems silent. Looking around from the
mountain top you can see forest plantations and the
scars ripped into them by logging and you can see the
pebble beaches on one coast and the sandy beaches
on the other. You can see the miniscule flags around
the cut and sculpted contours of the golf course and
the sandy bunkers in them like sun spots, the turrets
of the castle that welcome most of the tourists, and
the less welcoming peaks of the other of the islands
mountains, where brightly helmeted climbers the size
of figurines inch up the ragged sides on wisps of string.
The wildlife sees it all: the snakes among the grasses,

the insects on the plants and flowers, the birds of prey circling in the skies above the island and the surrounding shimmering fathoms of sea bright.

The house overlooking the bay is left like her parents had it. She put a sign up once but it fell down and she left it there on the lawn in the front garden. Without the job at the Co-op she probably wouldn't talk to anyone for days.

Twice a year a converted church is let for a week by a group of otherwise landlocked painters from Derbyshire. When they come in their ambling gangs to the Co-op she can never place the accent, only remember it from the time before, and she bags all their booze and smiles back at their smiles and wonders what goes on in the church. They are all sizes and ages: young lads who don't seem to wash and who drink all day every day, middle aged men in eccentric hats, fey wisps of men lost, others more obviously gay, in fact, almost completely defined by it, and then the women: middle aged gypsies wearing cheap jewellery and purple tents, young free girls with drunken hair and sated eyes, others uptight every year, others still just quiet and shy who bemoan leaving in intelligible voices without ever quite remembering her face.

They come summer and winter, and always there's one man the same, obviously the leader of the group. He always comes in on their first day and buys two crates of lager, carrying them out on his bulky shoulder. He is a big man who seems to get bigger every year, but like most of the painters he speaks in a gentle voice. It's the contrast between his bulk and his voice that draws her to him and the fact that he remembers

her face. All week long she sees him leading his paint-
erly band of stragglers along the coast road.

It seemed to be a regular thing for the youngest of
the boys to swim in the bay just across the road from
the Co-op, and if she could she'd go out on her break
and smoke a cigarette while seeming to look past the
half naked bodies towards the island of monks across
the bay. It made her smile how the women from the
groups studiously avoided looking at the boys in the
sea, and how the boys in the sea too obviously looked
over to the women before crashing headlong into wet
displays.

Once as she walked in the grounds of a castle she saw
the painters lined up with their canvasses in the sunlight and shadow of a battlement wall. They faced the
island across the bay, looking at a gap between tall trees
of sea, hill and sky from a grassy hillock where their
fold out chairs leaned at odd angles and the canvasses
themselves weren't level. She licked her ice cream and
watched from a bench as they alternately chatted and
concentrated, passing cans of lager between them and
growing progressively raucous as the canvasses filled
and the cans piled on the grass and the warm afternoon
lingered into a long evening where the puffballed sky-
scapes above the water were reflected on its burnished
surface. At one point a gypsy in purple fell off her seat
and rolled down the hill and the whole group laughed
as she did, laughed so long and so loud that eventually the crows in the tall trees above them croaked like
elderly neighbours. As the sun eventually set behind
the trees one or two kept painting and tried to capture
the changing light, while the others packed up and
walked from the castle grounds and back out on to the

coast road. She watched them the whole time and continued to do so when they stopped in the park overlooking the bay and unfolded their chairs and layed out
their canvasses side by side for inspection on the grass.
One of the painters, an ageing man with a moustache
and a white fedora, sat on one of the swings in the
park and began swinging out further and further. As
she watched from a bench by the bus shelter she saw as
the swing went higher and higher and faster and faster
so that it seemed to her that the chains would kink
and his swinging would end in disaster, but he kept
swinging even as his hat blew off and revealed his bald
head, swinging and swinging on into the darkness until
finally he fell off and rolled on the grass and one of the
young lads poured lager on him, a fountain of lager
causing him to jump up and then laugh and snatch
the can still laughing. The bus stopped and the driver
looked at her but she just gave him a nervous smile and
he hesitated before driving off and she watched again
across the darkness of a road unpolluted by street light
as the painters men and women in the park began to
strip down to their underwear before running into the
cold dark waters of the bay, some of them stripping to
nothing and cavorting through the shattered moonlight. She watched as the free young women spiralled
around with the gypsies and the young boys, looked
intently at the girls as they pulled off their tops with
their swinging and shining white breasts upraised as
they washed the wet hair back from their faces. Even
the big man jumped in with a tsunami splash and then
stood up tall from the shallows and roared his joy into
the island night.

Eventually a lugubrious policeman pulled up

parking carefully and approached the painters with his younger colleague and she watched from the bus shelter as the painters pretended to throw the older policeman into the water and offered him a can of lager before finally putting on their clothes again and beginning their walk back to the church. She sat in the bus shelter and felt that she'd been sweating, and she looked at her watch and realized it was way beyond the time she usually went to bed, and when she walked back in the moonlight, the road absent of all traffic and the only sound the washing of water against the shore, she felt a curious sense of novelty before dismissing it and hastening back to the house hoping the neighbours wouldn't see her.

Near the end of the week she saw that the painters were putting on an exhibition in the village hall and went along to have a look. The big man welcomed her with a hug and she was aware he'd been drinking. She walked past all the paintings, many of which were of landscapes familiar to her since childhood, but she lingered over the abstract things, though all the time conscious that someone or other was standing behind her, and she was sure she'd come back another day when all the people had gone.

When she went back the next day the room was empty save for bin liners filled with plastic cups and a cardboard box filled with empty wine bottles.

Loading up the shelves in the shop she'd forgotten to put the older loaves of bread at the front and her twenty year old supervisor noticed.

'We can't have this can we now?'

'What? Oh, sorry, sorry.'

'How long have you been here?'

'I know, I'm sorry,' she said, as the supervisor walked away, and she overheard the supervisor as she said to the girl on the till, 'she's hard work isn't she? Christ, it's not rocket science is it?' and the girl on the till smiled and the customer smiled.

She worked quickly to rectify the mistake and then went in the back and opened more boxes and came out with tins of soup and put them on the shelves, and when a customer dropped a bottle of milk and it split and leaked she mopped it up as other customers brushed past her.

On her break she sat smoking and overlooking the bay, wanting some swimmers to watch but not expecting any. She was hot from the work and the mistake and she thought how nice it might be to go into the water herself. But it was illogical. She had no swimming costume or towel. So instead she looked across at the island across the bay where the monks were, and where tourists could go across on a boat for ten pounds each.

The winter following she waited the painters arrival. But it was a harsh winter, the ferry cancelled more often than not. Snow covered the island across the bay for a while and the rest of the winter it almost always seemed to be raining and the lowering moodscapes of cloud traversed the skies in black frowns and furrows. At one point in April some kind of divinity airbrushed the moods in the window and a thin, tentative sunlight spread through the warming rooms of the house, lending life to fabrics seeming dead under the darkness of the winter months.

The summer she next expected the big man and his painting band they didn't come, and she never knew why. In the evenings she'd sit by the window in the upstairs bedroom and feel the wind from the bay blow across her ageing face and that was where she could have finished. But instead of sitting there to feel the evening wind she walked out into the moonlit night with a towel in her arm and a swimming costume on under her clothes. By the shoreline in the shadow of the swings she took off her clothes and folded them into a neat pile on the sand and paddled slowly out into the cold, cold water, turning back at first before thinking of the painters. She walked deeper and deeper into the water until she was up to her chin, and then she felt something run through her toes and so jumped off her feet and started swimming. The shock of it made her breathing heavy so that she swam back toward the shore and stood up again with the water at her waist and her chest falling and rising with the effort. Now she was in she didn't want to get out and swam faster to get warmer and something more than the water washed over her until she felt herself start to cramp and panicked a little and sloshed around and her head dipped under. With an effort she turned and made it back to the shore. And she walked out shivering and laughing from the water.

ACKNOWLEDGEMENTS

Some of these stories first appeared in the following magazines/zines: *The Bleed*, *Bottom of the World*, *Caledonian Review*, *Dreamcatcher*, *Glasgow Review*, *Horizon Review*, *Ink Sweat and Tears*, *Nutshell*, *Orbis*, *Pygmy Giant*, *Rainy City Stories*, *Spleen*, *Staple*, *Tomlit*, and *Unsung*—my thanks to the editors.

Lightning Source UK Ltd.
Milton Keynes UK
UKOW051407140212

187290UK00001B/4/P